Angel Eyes

Alex Westhaven

Angel Eyes
ISBN 9781937477851
Angel Eyes Copyright © 2011 Alex Westhaven
Published by Brazen Snake Books
All rights reserved.

Edited by Carol R. Ward
Cover art by Heidi Sutherlin

Chapter One

He watched from behind a tall Cyprus hedge as the lights came on in the small house across the street. Darkness had fallen hours ago, and Megan Hunter had finally come home. Her silhouette moved gracefully across the sheer curtains as she settled in and he admired the symmetry of her form. It was one of the things that had drawn his attention when he first saw her at the grocery store. She'd stepped out from behind the counter to help an elderly customer and he'd been stunned by the way her shoulders, breasts, hips and thighs all moved in a wonderfully artistic flowing curve. She'd looked up as he passed, a pleasant smile on her lips, but it was her eyes that had sealed her fate. They were beautiful, a toasted honey hue with just a hint of dark cinnamon flecks, like nothing he'd ever seen. He could just imagine what it would be like to look into those eyes every day, to have them look-

1

ing back at him. Perfection.

A warm breeze gusted, swirling red and gold leaves in playful patterns on the yard. He watched them float, his thumb absently rubbing the smooth leather case in one hand. Megan was in the kitchen now, sitting at a small table and tilting her head back for a long drink of water. He imagined caressing her long, slender throat, comparing it briefly in his mind to Angel's. Lovely as it was, it didn't quite measure up, but it didn't matter. That wasn't what he was here for.

She yawned and stretched. He checked his watch - it wouldn't be long now. She'd been thirsty, which worked in her favor. It was easier when they got a full dose. She rose, one hand to her mouth as she covered another yawn, and walked to the living room, stumbling past a chair and finally dropping out of his view. Excellent.

He slipped on a thin pair of leather gloves and waited another two minutes, then strode casually across the street and up her front steps. He inserted a key from his pocket into the lock and turned, the door swinging open easily. Closing and locking it behind him, he set his case down on the hall table beside her purse, snapped on a pair of latex gloves and went through the main rooms, closing all of the shades. He took his leather case into the master bathroom and laid out his tools on a clean towel, then carried Megan into the bathroom. He removed her clothes, folding them neatly and placing them on the laundry hamper next to the door before laying her in the bathtub. No reason to leave a mess behind for whoever found her.

She stirred, shivering as her skin puckered against the cool porcelain. Sitting on the edge of the tub, he tied a length of rubber tubing around her arm and waited for the veins to rise before slipping a needle into the largest. When the syringe was empty, he removed the tubing and placed it with the needle back in his case. He'd have to work fast now.

Quickly he changed his gloves and then opened one eyelid, and inserted a speculum to hold it away from the eyeball. He used a small set of forceps to pull the eye away from the socket, careful not to squeeze hard. Megan shuddered beneath him, and he frowned, hoping he'd given her enough to keep her still. Too late now, in any case. With his favorite scalpel, he quickly severed the optic nerve and placed the eyeball in a small jar of solution, then repeated the procedure on the other eye. He screwed the lid on the jar and wrapped his tools in plastic before returning them to the case. He'd clean them later, when he could do a good job. Megan whimpered, and he wasn't sure what to do. Normally they were dead by now - why was she still alive? For a moment he considered using the scalpel, but he hated to make more of a mess than necessary. Checking his watch again, he gathered up his things. He had morphine in the car. If he hurried, he could make it back with another dose before she became fully conscious.

He let himself out the back door and walked down the alley to the side street where he'd left his old Buick. Placing his kit in the spare tire compartment of the trunk, he filled the syringe and replaced the cap, then locked the car and jogged back down the alley with a grin. After he took care of Megan, he could spend the rest of the evening with Angel.

* * *

Jake had just dozed off when a loud chirping pulled him back from the edge of dreams. He rolled over, glancing at the alarm clock as he reached for the offending cell phone. A call at one in the morning was never good news, and he steeled himself for the worst as he put the piece to his ear.

"Dr. Werner," he said, rising to sit on the edge of the bed.

"Dr. Jacob Werner?" The female voice on the other end was cold, detached. Someone from the hospital, he guessed. He mentally flipped through the names of his near-suicidal patients, but they'd all been doing well this past week. Or so it had seemed. He ran a hand through his hair, stifling a yawn.

"Yes," he said, standing to reach for his pants. "Who is it? What happened?" Propping the small phone up with his shoulder at an awkward angle, he thrust one leg, then the other into tan khakis.

4

There was a pause on the other end while he zipped and buttoned. "Do you have a patient named Megan Hunter?"

He sat back down on the bed, nearly dropping the phone. Megan? She wasn't even a patient, just an intern, studying psychology and profiling at the local college while working a second job at the grocery store. She was smart, and very observant, which would serve her well in her chosen field.

"She works with me," he said, closing his eyes. "Is she going to be okay?"

"I'm sorry, Doctor - I can't discuss her case with anyone other than immediate family. We found your card in her wallet and thought you might know how we can reach someone for her."

Jake rubbed his forehead. "She doesn't have any immediate family. Who's the attending?"

"Doctor Stanik. But--"

"I'll be there in twenty minutes." He disconnected and slid the phone into his pocket, then pulled a t-shirt over his head. Topping it with a brown sport coat, he slipped his bare feet into a pair of brown leather loafers and grabbed his keys off the dresser.

"Where are you going?"

He looked back at the brunette sprawled half-naked in his bed and tried to remember her name. "I have to go to work. You're welcome to stay as long as you'd like though - just lock up when you leave."

"You're not going to call me, are you." Her statement halted him at the door and he paused for a moment. It was a trick question they both knew the answer to. He considered playing along for half a heartbeat.

"No."

* * *

Eighteen minutes later Jake jogged through the emergency room doors at Lindow General, swung left at the reception desk and slowed to a walk as he made his way down a long white corridor. The lights were dimmed, presumably for the comfort of sleeping patients, and the hallway deserted save one orderly pushing a linen cart. A right at the next corner, and he approached the ICU nurses station. Judging by the expression on the older blond at the desk, he was about to meet Ms. Cold and Detached in person. An unbidden shiver ran under his skin, and he fought the urge to look over his shoulder.

He leaned on the tall counter and held his right hand out. "Dr. Jacob Werner," he said, not really surprised when she didn't take his hand. "I'd like to speak with Dr. Stanik."

"He's not available at the moment, but there is someone here who'd like to speak with you. She's in room 1158, back down that hall, take a left and it should be on your left. Just go on in. She's expecting you." She took a stack of files off the counter and turned her back to him, effectively ending the exchange. Maybe Megan wasn't so bad off if she was up to visitors, but if that was the case, why had they been looking for next of kin?

He turned and retraced his steps, easily finding the correct room and pushing the door open to reveal a small blond dressed in an uptight black pantsuit standing at the head of a conference table. She looked up from the electronic tablet in her hand, peering at him over small wire-rimmed glasses before pushing them up farther on her nose.

"Dr. Werner - please have a seat."

He closed the door behind him, choosing a chair on the right side of the table, but not sitting. "Ladies first," he said, watching her closing for a reaction. She had to be in law enforcement, judging by the set of her shoulders, the uniform quality of her suit and the practical black shoes that did nothing for her feminine frame. He met her gaze, the cool green eyes unblinking as she watched him watching her. FBI, he guessed, and with that chip on her shoulder, probably one of the best. He pulled out the chair and sat down, satisfied with the look of surprise on her face, quickly hidden again behind her staid mask.

"I just have a few questions," she said. "I understand that Megan Hunter is one of your patients?" She paced the front of the room, her eyes trained on the tablet in her hand. He'd bet she wasn't reading anything, just acting the part.

"No."

She glanced up at him, as if she expected him to continue. When he didn't, she looked back at her file. "It says here that you worked with her - in what capacity did you know Megan?"

"She's an intern at my practice." This time when she looked at him, he raised an eyebrow, silently challenging her to work for the information she wanted.

To her credit, the woman merely looked back at the file. "What was the nature of your relationship?"

"I'm her boss," he replied, barely resisting the urge to expound. Something told him everything he said could and might be used against him. No reason to give them more ammunition than necessary.

Sliding into the head chair, the agent leaned forward. Jake appreciated the change in strategy when he caught an eyeful of smooth cleavage encased in lilac lace. "What color are Megan's eyes?"

"Hazel," he answered automatically, confused when the corner of her mouth curved up with just the slightest hint of satisfaction. He sat back in his chair, curious but wary.

"Where were you between eight and midnight tonight?" She slipped the glasses off, dangling them from one hand as she tilted her head. Apparently since the boob shot had worked, she figured flirtation was her best bet for information.

He played along, winking at her across the table. "At home, banging a curvy brunette I met at the bar.

I'm not planning on calling her again though, so if you're interested..." He stifled a laugh as the agent quickly put her glasses back on and sat up straight, all business again.

"I'll need her name, and the name of the bar you were at," she said, her voice ice cold. She pushed a notepad and pen across the table. "I'll also need a list of your patients, and anyone else who works with you."

He ignored the pen and paper. "The bar is O'Malley's on Thirteenth," he said, tired of playing. "I can't remember her name, and you'll need a warrant if you want information on any of my patients. Now, what the hell happened to Megan, and why can't I see her?"

"What color eyes does the ICU nurse have, Dr. Werner?"

Jake frowned at his interrogator as he recalled an image of the cold nurse's face. Cool blue eyes had matched her icy demeanor, if he remembered right. "Brown," he said, his gaze never wavering from hers. Somehow he sensed that a good memory for eye color was not an asset in this situation. Her eyes narrowed, holding his stare, and he was careful to stay relaxed. After a long moment she finally seemed to accept his answer and looked down to tap several spots on her electronic display.

"Megan was found earlier tonight in her bathroom. Only part of her was missing." She turned the device around, holding it up so he could see. "Is this your handiwork, Dr. Werner?"

It took a few seconds for his brain to process the image on the screen. He looked away as his stomach turned, threatening to empty itself all over the floor. He swallowed and took deep breaths, willing the nausea away. "Is she dead?" he asked, opting not to turn around. The motion of the chair could still be his undoing.

"No." Her chair creaked loudly and heels clicked across the floor as she came around the table, tablet in hand. "Are you okay?" The brusque tone was anything but caring, and he nodded, tapping down embarrassment. She held out a cell phone. "Call the woman you were with last night. Have her meet us at the Federal Building downtown. Once your alibi checks out, then we'll talk."

Jake shook his head, looking up at her. "You don't listen, do you Agent...what did you say your name was again?"

"I didn't."

"Well, whatever. I told you, I don't remember her name. I wasn't planning on calling her again, so I have no idea how to get a hold of her. So--"

Agent No-Name tapped one foot impatiently. "Do you have a nice house, Dr. Werner?"

He shrugged.

"Was she still at your house when you left?"

"Yes."

"Then call your house. I bet she's still there." She

dropped the phone in his lap and took two steps back.

He dialed, holding the phone to his ear. It rang three times before his answering machine picked up. "Uh...are you still there? Pick up the phone if you are - it's important." He let out the breath he hadn't realized he was holding as the line clicked.

"Jake?"

His date's voice was like music to his ear. "Yes, thank god you're still there. I have a little problem - remember that work thing?" Her wary response was less than reassuring. "Well, I was wondering if you could meet me downtown as soon as you can. At the Federal building."

A loud thud made him jerk the phone away from his ear. He disconnected and handed it back to the agent. "I think that was a no," he said, rubbing his neck with one hand.

The woman shook her head, one side of her mouth curving up just a bit. She dialed a number and held the phone to her ear. "How close are you to the Werner house? Good. There's a woman there, probably leaving as soon as she can. Pick her up and bring her in." She pushed one more button and slid the phone into the pocket of her jacket.

Jake stood. "Why didn't you just do that in the first place?" he asked, checking his watch. Two-fifteen in the morning, and it didn't look like he was going home anytime soon.

11

"Let's just call it research, and leave it at that." She went to the door and held it open. "After you."

He chuckled in disbelief. "Lady, I've played along this far, but you have to be crazy if you think I'm going anywhere with you without seeing some sort of identification."

She leaned against the door to keep it open and reached into her pocket, pulling out a black leather wallet. "Fair enough," she said, holding it open and up so he could read her credentials. Kate Paige, Special Agent to the FBI, as he'd suspected.

"Okay then, Agent Paige," he said, walking into the hallway. "I don't suppose I could see Megan for a minute before we leave?"

She fell into step beside him. "If your alibi checks out, someone will bring you back."

Chapter Two

Bright florescent lights filled the room with a low hum as the man flipped the wall switch. He closed the door behind him, snapping two deadbolts in place, quick, angry gestures at odds with his controlled demeanor. Carefully placing a small jar on the shiny white counter, he slipped paper covers over his shoes and a white paper cap over his head. Turning back to the wall he pushed a button, closing his eyes as the soothing strains of Bach eroded the frustration in his soul.

After several moments, he opened his eyes, reached for the jar and made his way between long spotless counters to the back wall of the lab. It took him ten minutes to gather everything he would need from the cabinets to the side, which he arranged on a silver tray lined with a white towel. When he was finished, he set the tray on a small wheeled table and rolled it over to his favorite chair beside a white block five feet long and three feet wide centered on the wall. It rose two feet off the floor, and the man took his seat on the right side. He leaned down to a control panel and inserted a small key. Several indicator lights glowed bright and he flipped three switches in succession, satisfied to hear gears working and moving behind the wall. The hiss of an air compressor fizzled as the wall began to move, the top of a large rectangle right above the block tilting inward as gears whined and moaned under the weight. The man rolled back a couple feet as the wall continued to fall, watching in appreciation as his Angel gradually came into view.

Her blond hair shone under the lab lights, reflecting it into a sort of halo as the wall-turned-table came to rest on the riser. Her porcelain skin never ceased to amaze him, so smooth and unblemished. He longed to touch it, to run his fingers over the alabaster surface, but he'd learned early not to give in to the temptation. Skin was hard to replace, and easily marred. He snapped on a pair of thin plastic gloves and stood to perform a quick evaluation. It had been awhile since he'd had Angel out of her case.

Reaching under her arm he tugged her dress free from the fasteners under the right side of her body, carefully shifting the thin fabric to pool at her left side. He examined her arms, torso, hips and legs for any sign of deterioration, paying extra attention to the suture sites. Relieved that everything looked okay, he moved to her other side and unhooked the clothing fasteners, tossing the dress into a round container to the side. Satisfied with the evaluation of her left side, he checked her feet, cursing when he found torn spots on the bottom of each. They'd have to be replaced, of course, and he made a mental note. It was time to schedule another manicure. Maybe if he shortened the ankles this time, they wouldn't press so hard against the bottom of her case.

Her knees, thighs and pelvis were perfect, just as he'd installed them and he smiled at the memory of their donors. Lovely women, all three, and he'd been lucky to find them together one night. Higher, her stomach and rib cage were slim, but not skinny, and her perfect breasts lay slightly higher than normal due to the tight skin that kept them straight and shapely without a bra when she was upright. He moved his hand over her, not touching, but close enough to feel the gentle warmth coming off her skin. It had taken him so long to perfect that little detail.

Glancing up at her chest, he timed the movements as it rose and fell, softly as if she were sleeping. The effect was barely noticeable when she was upright, but it added another layer of realness to her demeanor that he rather liked. He'd tried to sell the technology he'd developed to toy makers, but of the few who had been interested, none had wanted to pay his price. Holding his hand over her mouth, he felt the gentle breaths that would make a pattern on the glass when

15

the room was cold. The sutures around her lips were still slightly visible, but he'd only installed the new pair two weeks ago. It took time for the skin to adjust to the new shape.

He checked her ears and scalp quickly, anxious to move on. Finally he looked into her eyes, sighing at the broken vessels and pocked surface. He'd come so far, and yet everything came back to the eyes. She required a new pair every six weeks or so, because he hadn't yet figured out how to preserve them well enough to survive in the same environment her skin liked inside the case. Not that it mattered. He never could seem to find the perfect color, and while it was taxing to replace them, he was tired of the jeweled green color he'd chosen last time. He reached back for the jar, holding it up to the light as Megan's hazel irises stared back. He grinned, setting the jar beside Angel's head and picking up a speculum.

"Don't worry, darling," he murmured as he carefully braced one eyelid open. "You'll be beautiful again soon."

* * *

Jake refrained from drumming his fingers on the table. It was nerve-wracking, sitting alone in a cold interrogation room with only the standard-issue mirrored window for company. He considered all the guilty confessions that had probably been made in this very room, and wondered how many of them were given due to a heightened state of anxiety like he was experiencing now. Before he'd always considered the method somewhat unfair to the innocent, and his opinion hadn't changed in the past hour he'd been left to stew in his own thoughts. The urge to get up and pace, to check his watch, hell, do anything besides sit quietly was like a bad itch that couldn't be reached. But he remained still, knowing the people on the other side of the mirror were watching for any behavior at all that could be construed as guilty.

Finally, the door knob turned and Agent Paige stepped into the room. She took the chair across from him, tapping a finger on that electronic pad that seemed glued to her hand. "Well Dr. Werner, it looks like your alibi checks out. I do have just a few more questions though..."

Yeah, right. He maintained a neutral expression and nodded, indicating for her to continue. Her eyes narrowed an expression she probably didn't even realize she was making as she started at him for a few more seconds. He nearly laughed at her confusion. He'd always liked manipulating people. It was an endless source of free amusement.

"Do you specialize in any one field of study, Doctor?" She cocked her head to the side, probably trying for conversational. He considered telling her similar moves had never worked for him, but she didn't look like a rookie. Maybe he should ask her how it worked in interrogation. Clearly it wasn't working just now.

"Compulsive behaviors," he finally answered, intrigued when she merely nodded. Most people instinctively took stock of themselves, self-consciously drawing attention to whatever habit they wished to hide. Agent Paige merely made a note on the tablet screen.

"How many patients do you have, approximately?"

He hesitated, not wanting to answer too quickly. "Twenty-five," he said, once again receiving only a nod. It occurred to him that she already knew the answers, and was fishing for something. But what?

"What color eyes do I have?"

There it was. He remained silent, waiting until she finally looked up. "Green," he said, his gaze never leaving hers. Suddenly it came together in his mind, and he leaned forward. "The bastard took Megan's eyes," he said, glancing down at the table as he reluctantly pictured the image she'd shown him in his head. "And you think that whoever took them wanted a specific color."

She shook her head, staring at him for a long moment. "Your alibi checked out, though I don't think that woman wants to see you again. We also got a call from someone who speaks very highly of you. He suggested we consult with you on this case."

Jake tried to think of someone he knew with that much clout, but couldn't. "Who?"

"A former patient who claims you treated him for

something when you were first starting out. Apparently he's friends with some people pretty high up in the food chain, though he asked to remain anonymous." Her expression was relaxed, but the tense set of her shoulders said she wasn't comfortable with the situation. Jake couldn't blame her. There was something odd about getting a recommendation from someone he must have treated at least ten years ago. Still, the case was intriguing, and he wanted to help find whoever took Megan's eyes. He braced his forearms on the table, lacing his fingers together.

"Looks like I'm all yours then." He pointed at the device in her hand. "What do we know about this guy?"

Agent Paige shifted in her seat, leaning back to regard him with narrowed eyes. *Here it comes*, he thought, holding back a grin. Insecurity often plagued even the strongest individuals, and he suspected a lecture on boundaries was on the way.

"I thought maybe we'd try an experiment first, if you don't mind. I'm more curious to find out what we don't know than to rehash what we do, to be honest."

Jake nodded, intrigued that she chose a test rather than a lecture. Not insecurity then, but caution. "Whatever I can do to help."

She turned the screen around, and called up an image, pushing it to him. "This is from the first crime scene we connected to the perpetrator. We think he killed four women before attacking Ms. Hunter. All five crimes were very similar, including your intern's though she was the only one left alive. What can you tell me about the him based on this?"

He peered down at the screen, consciously avoiding looking at the dark shape at the right edge just yet. "All of the killings were done in the bathroom?"

"Yes."

"It's very clean," he said, using his fingers to zoom in and out of different areas of the photo. "Not even water spots on the faucets. I don't know anyone who keeps their bathroom that clean." There was a laundry hamper in the corner, with a lid. "Did you find anything in the hampers?" He glanced up in time to see a glint of appreciation in Agent Paige's expression.

"Just the clothing the victim had been wearing that day."

"Interesting." He turned his attention to the victim then, lying naked in a white porcelain bathtub. A white towel lay folded neatly on the edge next to her head, apparently unused. He frowned, remembering the pale red stains he'd seen on Megan's face in her photo. "Where's the blood?"

"There normally isn't any by the time we get there."

He looked over the body, the skin smooth and unmarred. "There are no bruises, no marks...she didn't fight?"

"None of them did."

Jake sat back, crossing his arms over his chest. "From what I see here, I'd say the killer is a neat freak

- obsessively so. Which means it's highly unlikely he'll ever leave a fingerprint or hair behind."

Paige shrugged, clearly finding his assessment boring. "We know that. What can you tell us that we don't know?"

He thought for a moment. "It's not a lot of information to go on, but my guess is that he - or she - is also a perfectionist. He takes great care in choosing his victim, and then plans the event for days, maybe even weeks before the actual attack. He probably lives in a nice house, maybe even employs a cleaning service, though they'll never do as good a job as he requires. He's well-groomed, and would target those who obviously take care with their own appearance."

Scribbling notes on a small pad of paper, Paige didn't even glance up. "Go on."

"That kind of obsession would require at least a middle-class income, so the killer is either independently wealthy, taken care of by someone, or holds down a job of some sort. It would be hard for him to hold down a job though, due to his obsessive nature. He'd have to be very good at hiding it."

Paige put down the pen, her lips curving up in the closest thing he'd seen to a smile. "Very impressive, Dr. Werner. We--"

"Jake, please."

"As I was saying, Dr. Werner, we'll add this to the file. If you'd like to visit your intern now, I can have someone take you back to the hospital. We'll call if we need anything further."

Jake sat back, trying to recall anything he might have missed. Apparently he'd failed the test, but he wasn't sure how.

The door opened and a tall, nearly bald man with a gray mustache peered around it. "Agent Paige, a word?"

* * *

Half an hour later, Jake followed Agent Paige down the darkened corridor of the hospital again. Whatever the man had said to her had pissed her off good, and he wondered if she was really the best person to question Megan right now. They turned onto the ICU ward, where his favorite nurse stood glaring behind the desk. *This should be fun.*

"I didn't expect either of you back here," she said pointedly. "I thought I made it clear that no visitors--"

"It's okay, Shauna. I called them."

Jake nodded at the tall, slender man who stepped through the office doorway behind the nurse. "Thanks Will. I'm glad it's you taking care of her. How's she doing?"

"Come on, I'll show you." The doctor joined them in front of the desk, leading the way down a shorter side hall. "She's still sedated, but she's been waking up on and off, scared. I thought it might help to hear a familiar voice." He stopped in front of a large glass

22

window, motioning for them to look through.

A dim florescent light above her bed gave off just enough of a glow for Jake to make out the small figure lying there. Her eyes, or where they should be, were covered with white gauze, and he fought back the memory of those images Paige had shown him earlier. "Does she know what happened?"

Will shook his head. "She hasn't been coherent for any length of time yet. And since you were the contact, I thought it might be better if she heard it from you."

"How do you two know each other?"

Jake turned. He'd nearly forgotten about Paige. "We went to college together, shared a place for awhile." Her eyes narrowed, and he grinned. "No. Don't even go there. Will's memory is worse than mine, and he never looks women in the eye. He saves lives, he doesn't take them." He glanced at Will, who was pretending to study something on the chart in his hands, then back at Paige, also peering down at her tablet. He rubbed his neck, tired and wanting to be anywhere else. "Can I go in and see her now?"

"Sure. Just keep it low-key, okay? I'll be back in twenty minutes - that should be enough for tonight."

"Thanks." Jake pushed open the door and walked to Megan's side, the sound of Paige's footsteps echoing softly behind. He stroked Megan's arm gently a few times, until she stirred, her head moving side to side.

23

"Who are you? Where am I? Why can't I see?" Her hands rose off the bed, reaching for...something as her cries grew frantic.

"Sssh, Megan. It's Dr. Werner. You need to lie back and I'll tell you everything." He grasped her hands, her fingernails digging into his flesh as she gripped him tightly. "That's it, hold on to me," he said, pitching his voice low and soothing.

Megan lay back against the pillow, her breathing shallow. "My eyes," she whimpered, tugging at him. "Why can't I see?"

Jake glanced over his shoulder at Agent Paige, realizing he didn't actually know the whole story. She stood at the foot of the bed, her unfeeling gaze locked on the girl. She'd probably seen victims in worse shape, he thought as he turned back to his intern. There wasn't time to get the details now. He had to get this over with so Megan could start coming to terms with her new reality.

"You were attacked," he said, shifting to hold both of her hands in one of his so he could stroke her forehead with the other. "The person who did this...he didn't intend to let you live. I'm so sorry, Megan, but he took your eyes."

Chapter Three

"There you go, Angel. Good as new." Peeling off a pair of gloves, the man tossed them into a red garbage bag attached under the rolling tray and snapped on a clean, dry pair. He leaned down and pulled a drawer in the white slab open, rifling through bits of fabric and lace until he found just the right pieces. "It's getting cooler out, dear. Something warmer than a sundress, I think."

He closed the drawer and stood, then carefully laid a pair of jeans over her legs, attaching them to the fasteners on the platform just under each leg and around her hips. He repeated the process with a rust-colored sweater to match her new eyes, and a jaunty matching beret to finish the look. Moving to her feet he carefully added a pair of argyle socks topped with brown loafers. Those feet really did need to be replaced.

25

Checking his watch, he cursed. Angel had been out of her case for three minutes longer than ideal - an oversight that may well cost her some skin. Skin was his least-favorite part to collect, so delicate and prone to drying. He ripped off the gloves and bent down to flip a couple switches, finally pressing a green button. The head of the platform rose at a slow, steady pace, carrying Angel back into the environment he'd created especially for her. Her blond hair glistened in the bright lights until finally she disappeared from view, the opening sealed with a long hissing noise. He wanted to go see her, and watch her new eyes shine as he told her about Megan and how he'd let her live. About the psychologist she worked with when she wasn't checking groceries. The same psychologist who had helped him realize his true potential. Angel was a good listener.

He turned off the panel on the white riser, then pushed the wheeled tray to the large sinks in the center of the counter. Angel would have to wait while he cleaned the lab. He turned on the water in one sink and plugged the drain, placing his tools neatly on the bottom of the basin. Careful to keep his hands clear of the near-boiling stream from the tap, he squirted a thick solution from a clear plastic bottle into the water. When the level was high enough to cover the utensils, he swung the high tap to the second sink and let it run down the drain, reaching back for the small glass bowl holding two cloudy green eyes. Tilting the bowl, he let the offending appendages roll into the automatic disposal and listened to the satisfying growl as it chewed and swallowed. The dish went into the other basin and he turned the water off, reaching for a long pair of thick gloves that hung on a rack above the sinks.

Hands well protected, he scrubbed each item thoroughly before placing it neatly on a steel rack beside the sink. When the sink was empty, he pulled the plug, rinsing the shiny interior as well as the gloves. He replaced the spray nozzle and turned off the water, hanging the gloves back above the sink. Then he rolled the metal rack into a large square box and secured the door, pushing a button to start the industrial dishwasher.

Another thin pair of gloves covered his hands as he sprayed a clear liquid onto the counters and the rolling tray, where it bubbled on contact before he wiped it off with a thick sponge. He worked outward from there, spraying and wiping every flat surface in the room, unable to stop until every inch had been touched. The bottle put away, he tossed the sponge and gloves into the garbage bag, then touching only the outside he detached the bag and secured the top with a plastic tie. Turning in a circle, he examined the room, and finally satisfied he went to the door and punched in the code to let himself out. A quick trip downstairs to his private garbage collection bin, and he'd be free to join Angel in the study for a drink.

* * *

Jake gratefully took the cup of coffee Agent Paige handed him, and peered through the half-closed blinds of Megan's hospital room. She'd been inconsolable after he told her about the attack, and Stanik had given her a sedative to calm her down. Paige had left for awhile, leaving a bodyguard behind in case the killer decided to finish the job.

"Has she woken up yet?" Paige joined him at the window.

He took a sip of the hot brew and checked his watch. "Not yet, but should be anytime. Stanik said a couple of hours, and it's nearly eight." Paige nodded, her expression thoughtful.

"Do you think she'll be okay to talk when she wakes up? We could really use a lead here, and she's our only hope."

Shifting his weight to one foot, he shrugged. "No way to know, really. She's always seemed like a strong person to me, but with something like this...it's a pretty big adjustment to realize that you'll never see again." He noticed Megan's head move to the side a little. "Looks like we're about to find out."

He pushed open the door and went in, setting his coffee on the table at the foot of the bed. "Megan? It's Dr. Werner." She raised a hand, searching the air and he took it in his, surprised at the strength in her trembling fingers.

"My eyes hurt." She reached up with her other hand, pressing at the bandages on her face. Jake reached over and pressed the call button. "How can they hurt if..." she didn't finish the sentence, and Jake squeezed her hand.

"The nurse will be here soon - she'll give you something for the pain." He glanced at Agent Paige, her electronic tablet in one hand. "Megan, there's an FBI agent here with me, and we'd like to ask you some questions. Is that okay?"

She hesitated, then slowly nodded. "I really don't remember anything though. The last thing I remember is sitting down to eat dinner after work." She turned her head toward Jake. "I worked late at the store last night. I got home around eight-thirty, I think."

"The store?" Agent Paige asked, frowning. "I thought you worked with Dr. Werner?"

Jake stroked Megan's hand. "She interns with me in the morning, and works as a checker at Thrifty Dee's in the afternoon."

Paige nodded. "Did anything unusual happen at the store last night? Anyone approach you that you don't know?"

"No, nothing like that. It was quiet, actually. The only people who came in were a few regulars." She shifted restlessly. "My eyes really hurt..."

"What about before? Do you remember anything

strange happening at the store in the past few weeks? Someone who made you nervous, maybe?"

"I don't know...I can't..." Megan shifted again, her grip on Jake's hand nearly cutting off the circulation.

Jake shot Paige a warning glare. "Shh...it's okay Megan. We can do this later."

The door opened and a nurse breezed in, her face stern and pale. "I see our patient is awake. How are you feeling?"

"My eyes hurt. Bad." The catch in the girl's voice belayed how close to crying she was. "How can they hurt when they're gone?"

The nurse adjusted a switch on the IV, and pushed a button on the stand. "I'll let the doctor explain in detail, but basically your nerves are pretty upset at being detached, so they're going to complain for awhile. We'll do our best to keep you comfortable." She glanced at Jake and Paige. "I'll need to ask you to leave while we attend to some personal matters..."

"Sure," Jake said. He squeezed Megan's arm lightly. "I'll be back tonight, okay?"

Megan nodded. He was almost to the door when she called out. "Wait - there was one guy..."

He turned, Agent Paige bumping his arm as she moved back into the room. "A guy? What was unusual about him?" she asked.

Megan took in a deep breath, then let it out slowly. She rolled her head to the side, as if looking at them. "He gave me a compliment. He said I had beautiful eyes."

* * *

Jake stifled a yawn as he got in the passenger side of the dark FBI issue sedan. Agent Paige slid behind the steering wheel and started the engine, glancing briefly in his direction.

"I'm taking you home," she announced as she backed out of the parking spot. "You haven't slept all night, and you're no good to anyone in that state."

He frowned, illogically annoyed by the statement. "I don't need to go home. If you're going to work, I want to help." The look she gave him wasn't one of irritation as he'd expected, but rather one of amusement.

"You sound like a petulant child." She turned left at the next light, and Jake recognized his own street. "I'm just going to call the store Ms. Hunter worked at, and have them send over the security tapes for the last few weeks. I figure we should be able to recognize him well enough. I'm sure it will be several hours though. You have time to take a nap and grab a shower. I'd suggest you take advantage of the opportunity now."

Jack nodded and rubbed his neck as she pulled the car into his driveway. "I am tired," he admitted, pushing the door open. "Call me when the videos come in?"

31

Paige shook her head. "Why don't you just get a good night's sleep and come in tomorrow morning. By then I should have something for you to look at."

Too tired to argue, Jake shrugged. "Fine. I'll see you then."

He watched her pull out of the driveway then went to the door, swearing under his breath when the door swung open as he tried to insert the key. Wondering whether his date had been pissed at his easy dismissal or just in a hurry, he closed the door and snapped the deadbolt shut. Turning, he nearly impaled his foot on an abandoned stiletto. She'd been in a hurry, then. He picked up the shoe and placed it by the door before continuing on to the kitchen. He tossed his keys on the counter and made his way down a short hall to the master suite, greeted by a rumpled bed and a folded piece of paper on his pillow. For a long moment he just stood there, contemplating the potential contents as he shucked his clothes and tossed them in the general vicinity of the laundry hamper. Why some women felt the need to explain every single thought in their head was beyond him, and he didn't particularly feel up to dealing with that sort of drama. He left the note where it lay, and padded across the room to the bathroom. A shower first, then sleep.

He turned the water on and stepped under the spray, wincing a little at the heat against his skin. Adjusting the temperature, he closed his eyes and let the water run down over his head as the images he'd analyzed cycled through his head. Emotions warred within as he silently acknowledged a certain fascination with the killer. Almost certainly a man, he thought, considering the methodical and almost merciful execution of each job. He hadn't really studied criminology before, but women tended to act on emotion, and from what he'd seen, these murders were more about getting what the killer needed, rather than the actual taking of a life. But what would anyone need with several sets of human eyes, all different colors?

He toweled off and went back to the bedroom, dropping the towel on the floor as he sat on the edge of the bed. Picking up the note, he considered throwing it away unread. His curiosity won, and he unfolded the note. A phone number was scrawled at the top, with one line underneath.

"I need to consult with you on an important business matter. Please call me."

Frowning at the paper in his hand, Jake automatically reached for his phone. There was no evidence anyone else had been in the house, but he hadn't told the woman his profession last night, so why would she want to talk about business? Unless she was a prostitute. But that probably would have come out at the police station. He grinned at the thought of what the cool Agent Paige would have thought about that.

Digital notes to a popular song began playing in his hand, and he looked at the number on the screen. His office number came up, and he winced, remembering the appointments he'd meant to call and have Edith reschedule. She was the best office manager he'd ever had, but last minute scheduling changes tended to send her into a panic. Pushing a button, he held the device to his ear. "Edith, I'm so sorry --"

"Oh that's quite alright, dear. A nice young lady from the FBI called earlier this morning and said you wouldn't be in today. So I re-scheduled your appointments for next week. She was asking about Megan - what happened? Are you okay?"

Jake sighed, closing his eyes and rolling his head from side to side. "I'm fine. Megan's in the hospital, but she'll be okay eventually. I'll tell you all about it later. So what was it you needed then?"

"Well, another woman's been calling for you, and it sounds quite urgent. She's called three times now, and wants to schedule an appointment but she says she can't wait until your next open spot in three weeks. I tried to give her a referral to another office, but she insists that it has to be you. I'm not sure what to do now."

He rubbed a hand through his hair, stifling another yawn. "I'll give her a call - what's her number?" He grabbed a pen and the note off the nightstand, and jotted the number down as Edith rattled it off. It looked very familiar, for some reason.

"And her name is Angela Redding."

He nodded, unable to hold back yet another yawn. "Got it. Thanks Edith, I'll call her. Feel free to close up early if you'd like since I'm not seeing anyone today, and it's probably best if you reschedule tomorrow's appointments too."

After he disconnected the call, he looked at the number again. He turned the paper over, and sure enough, the numbers matched. Assuming that the woman in his bed last night had been Angela Redding, he was curious why she hadn't said anything before. He punched her number into his phone for the second time and was just about to connect when the doorbell rang.

So much for that nap.

Quickly pulling on a pair of sweats and a t-shirt, he went to the door and opened it, not surprised to see his recent bed mate standing on the front step, all business in a black skirt suit and red shirt with what looked like a yearbook tucked in the crook of one arm. "Angela Redding, I presume?"

She nodded. "I'm sorry to bother you, but this really can't wait. May I come in?"

"Of course." He stepped aside, closing the door after her and leading her into the living room. "Can I get you something to drink?"

She shook her head, taking a seat on the couch. "No thank you." She set her purse on the floor and the book on the table, resting one hand lightly on the cover. "Dr. Werner, I need to apologize for my...*forward* behavior last night. I had no idea who you were, and if I had, I assure you, I would have conducted myself more...professionally."

Jake sat in the armchair across from her, bracing his elbows on his knees. "No apologies necessary - last night wasn't exactly planned for me either, so we'll call it even. But I hope you understand that I can't take you on as a client now."

Her eyes widened, and she shook her head again. "Oh, no. I don't need that type of professional help. Well, I do, or I did, but I have--had a therapist ..." She closed her eyes and took a deep breath, letting it out slowly before she stared at the book in front of her.

"Five years ago, I was kidnapped and held for three weeks before I escaped. I don't remember much of the time I spent there, but I think I know who did it. He's smart. Really smart, and rich, and no one could ever find any evidence to convict him, since I couldn't provide a positive ID. I changed my appearance and my name, and I've spent the last several years trying to figure out how to prove he's the one who took me." She paused, glancing up to look Jake in the eye. "I think this man was one of your patients, and if what I've seen him doing lately is any indication, he's up to something a lot worse than kidnapping these days."

Chapter Four

Floor-to-ceiling bookshelves were illuminated by soft yellow light as the man entered the library. He walked across the room to stand in front of a long, dark brown velvet drape hanging over the front of a section of shelves. Reaching around the left edge of the curtain, he pushed a button and stepped back to watch the fabric panels part. There, encased in an extra large display box was his Angel, her chest moving in and out ever so slightly as her "breath" played against the window. He'd decided on a quick nap after cleaning the lab, and was glad now that he had waited to visit. They had so much to discuss.

"Good evening, my dear. That sweater really does look lovely on you. And those eyes - I knew they would be the perfect shade." He leaned closer to the glass, squinting as he looked carefully into each one. The clear gel he'd painstakingly brushed over the surface was still too shiny, and he sighed. "A little thinner coat next time, I guess."

He turned and went to his favorite chair, a wide leather cigar model with a matching ottoman. As he required, a cut-glass decanter filled exactly half-way with brandy sat on the small table to his right, along with a clean tulip glass. He poured two fingers and replaced the bottle stopper, swirling the deep maroon liquid around and around in the glass as he put his feet up.

"I told you about Miss Hunter, of course. She was good at first, and didn't put up a fight. You know I don't like to hurt them, but she ... there was something different about her." He sipped from the glass, his brows pulled together in thought. "The drugs ... the normal dose wasn't enough to keep her asleep. I barely had time to collect your eyes and then, well ..." he took another sip, staring at his feet. "Someone found her before I could finish. She's still alive, Angel. I failed." His eyes blurred as he swallowed the last of his drink and set the glass aside. Hands folded in his lap, he tried to collect his scattered thoughts.

"I don't know what to do about her," he said finally, moving his feet off the ottoman and leaning forward, elbows braced on his knees. "Living without sight will be a difficult adjustment. I can set up a fund for her, but it just doesn't seem right to leave her...like that." He sighed, sitting up to run a hand through his hair. "I wonder how Murray's research is coming. Perhaps he has something that might help. I think I'll give him a call, maybe order a gift for our dear Miss Hunter. It's really the least I can do."

He settled back in the chair, and poured another drink. "Do you remember that doctor I told you about? The one who taught me how to control my impulses? As it turns out, Miss Hunter was interning for him part time. Small world, isn't it? From what I hear, my brother has requested Dr. Werner's consulting services on my case, which could be fun for awhile, as long as he doesn't get too close. Although I am curious about what he would think of you. In a way, you were his idea, after all."

Setting his drink aside unfinished, he stood. "I should go check on that gift for Miss Hunter." He approached the case and squatted to examine her feet, shaking his head. "There's a big fundraiser at Todd's place tomorrow night, formal dress. There should be some promising replacement options on display."

* * *

Jake thumbed through the black book Angela had brought while she sat on the edge of the couch, biting her thumbnail. She was definitely nervous, and he wondered again why she hadn't gone straight to the police instead of coming to him. He put the book down, the little bits of information she'd uncovered over the past five years painting a potentially grim picture of Trent Abernathy, the man she believed had kidnapped her. He also happened to be the son of a wealthy former-senator, which could explain why the police hadn't pressed the issue with no hard evidence to go on.

"What makes you think he was one of my patients?" He'd recognized the name right away - the senator had paid very good money for an intensive therapy program for his son, and Jake considered Abernathy one of his earliest successes, even though patient confidentiality agreements kept him from sharing the details of the case.

Angela opened the book to a page near the end, where she'd taped some newspaper clippings. "Trent's disorder was mentioned a couple of times in the society pages when people noticed him doing odd things in public, like wiping down counters, rearranging furniture and dishes, and of course not wanting any physical contact with others. Then he sort of disappeared for awhile, and when he resurfaced, those behaviors were either gone or diminished." She turned the page, pointing to Jake's name on a list. "I called around, and there were only three therapists in town that had the skills to help someone like that. I called the other two, and they didn't have any record of Trent as a patient, so here I am."

Careful to keep his expression neutral, he sat back in the chair, lifting one ankle to rest on the opposite knee. "I'm sure you realize that if Abernathy was ever a patient of mine, I wouldn't be able to talk about his case with you. So what is it that you want from me, exactly?"

She nodded, closing the book. "I was hoping that perhaps you'd make an exception considering the circumstances..." He shook his head. "In that case, what I'd like you to do is tell me, hypothetically, how an obsessive/compulsive person could learn to use his or her disorder to become a serial killer."

Jake rubbed a hand on the side of his neck. "I don't think you realize the enormity of that question." He leaned forward, propping his arms on his knees again. "And even if I could make a hypothetical case, that's all it would be. It wouldn't get you any closer to real evidence you can use." He paused, examining the dark circles under her eyes that she'd almost hidden with makeup, the absolute weariness in her gaze. "Have you considered the possibility that the lengths you've gone to in trying to prove Abernathy guilty could be a form of OCD?"

Her eyes narrowed, hardening her expression as she reached for the book with one hand, and her purse with the other. "Thank you for your time, Dr. Werner. I'm sorry to have wasted it." She stood and walked past him out of the living room, her heels clicking on the hardwood floor. Jake considered going after her, but forced himself to stay where he was, not wanting to encourage her. Not yet, at least. He waited until the front door closed and padded back to the

41

bedroom, considering his bed for a moment. Abernathy had been a particularly difficult case, and he remembered a few snippets of conversation during their sessions that had been...disturbing. In light of the conversations he'd had today with Agent Paige and now Redding, it wouldn't hurt to take a closer look. Cursing under his breath, he got dressed and grabbed his keys, making sure the front door was locked as he left.

* * *

Two hours later, Jake tossed another brown file folder onto the stack on his desk. Abernathy had come to him for eighteen months, but nothing really stood out in the notes he'd taken during their sessions. One of his main issues had been the need for a nearly sterile environment, and while there wasn't really any way to cure it, Jake had helped him channel the compulsion into productive, efficient cleaning methods to minimize the time spent satisfying the need. Abernathy was a perfectionist, and Jake had been able to help him control his reactions to imperfections he couldn't control, which had helped Abernathy to at least appear less judgmental than he really was. That's what the therapy had primarily focused on - retraining Abernathy to hide his natural compulsions while with other people.

For the most part, it had been successful. Jake remembered the last session, when Abernathy had thanked him eloquently and shaken his hand as if it was perfectly normal. Jake had known that Abernathy would apply sanitizer once he was out of sight, but the fact that he could keep his reaction under control until later just proved the therapy had worked. He'd told Abernathy to call if he needed anything else, and sent him on his way.

Jake frowned, leaning forward to shuffle through the files again. Abernathy had called after that, just once several years later. He reached the bottom of the stack, then went over them again, not finding the one he needed. Maybe he'd overlooked a box when he was retrieving the files. He yawned, glancing at his watch as he walked to the storage room. It was nearly six, but it felt like midnight, and he yawned again as he unlocked the door and flipped on the light. Cheap cardboard boxes waited on open metal shelving, and he went to the place he'd removed the Abernathy box from. The boxes on either side of the space were labeled with the generic "AB" and "AC" that denoted more than one patient file inside. He opened the "AB" box, and thumbed through the contents, finding a lone file marked "Abernathy" at the very back. He pulled it out and closed the box, quickly scanning the pages as he walked back to his office.

He sat behind his desk, concern growing as he read through the five year old transcript. Abernathy had just broken up with a girlfriend, the first relationship he'd had for longer than a couple of days. He'd been agitated and nearly suicidal, begging Jake to help him figure out how to get the woman back. His angel, he'd called her, and the session had run nearly three hours while Jake had helped calm him down enough to start the healing process.

Angel. Angela. Jake sat back in his chair, considering the implications of what he'd found. He rubbed his forehead, unsure how to proceed. He still didn't have any proof that Angela Redding was the angel Abernathy had broken up with, or if she was that he'd kidnapped her. Everything was still speculation at this point, though the file did seem to suggest a possible connection.

The sound of a door opening out front brought his gaze to the office window. He'd locked the door when he came in, and his secretary and Megan were the only other people with keys. Setting the file with the others he took his phone off the desk and went to investigate, curious to find the front door locked when he tried it. He made a quick sweep of the office, checking the back door as well and then went back to his desk. Obviously the lack of sleep was taking its toll, and he shook his head at his overactive imagination. He'd take the file home and go over it in more detail there after a good nap. He glanced at the surface of his desk, annoyed when the file wasn't where he thought he left it. He looked through the stack, and when it wasn't there, in his drawers and on the floor. He checked the front office again and retraced his steps through the suite to no avail.

The file was gone.

Jake retrieved Agent Paige's card from his wallet and started putting her number in his phone when a call came in from the same. He pushed the button to answer. "Agent Paige, I was just going to call you--"

"The hospital called," she said, cutting him off. There was an odd note in her voice, and he sat in his chair, the file forgotten.

"Megan...is she okay?"

"In a manner of speaking. She's okay physically, but..." The agent paused, and he could almost imagine the wheels turning in her brain, trying to decide how much to tell him over the phone. He stood, patting his pocket to make sure his keys were there.

"Where should I meet you?" He strode quickly out the back door, taking the time to make sure the deadbolt was locked and the alarm system armed.

"At the hospital."

He shoved his phone back in his pocket and drove to the hospital as fast as he could, narrowly avoiding two accidents on the way. Walking quickly down the now-familiar corridor, he stopped just outside Megan's room, peering through the window. Agent Paige was standing by her bed, holding her hand. In the other hand was a small box. As if she sensed him, she glanced over her shoulder, nodding him in. He pushed the door open, alarmed to hear his intern's breath coming in short gasps.

"Dr. Werner's here, Megan." Agent Paige stepped back, releasing her hand.

He wrapped his fingers around hers and half-sat on the bed, leaning close to her tear-stained face. "Shh...it's okay. I'm here." He stroked her hair back, frowning. "Can you tell me what happened? Did someone hurt you?"

She rolled her head back and forth across the pillow. "A man came to see me. He..." she sniffed, and took a deep breath. "He told me I was very lucky to survive the attack, and that he was sorry I had to live th-this way." She paused again. "He gave me a box, and told me to open it. I did, and I felt inside...oh god." Her free hand came up to cover her mouth as she cried fresh tears.

Jake squeezed her hand, caressing her face until she quieted. "You don't have to say anything more. I just need to talk to Agent Paige in the hall for a few minutes, okay?"

"Okay." Megan squeezed his hand when he tried to withdraw, letting him go at the last possible second. "Will you come back?"

"Of course." He followed Paige into the hall, looking pointedly at the box as soon as the door shut behind them. "Do you think it was him?"

She shook her head. "I don't think he'd risk getting so close, even as meticulous as he is. Definitely someone he knows though. Someone with connections." She held the box out to him, and he reached to take it, then pulled his hand back.

"What about fingerprints?"

She shrugged. "At least a few people on the staff touched it before I even got here, plus the guard I assigned to watch her. I doubt we'll get anything useful off of it, small as it is. Just don't touch the contents."

He took it, using his thumb to pry the lid open. "Where was the--wow." He lowered himself into a nearby chair, staring at the contents. Nestled in what looked like black velvet were two gleaming eyes staring up at him, the same distinctive amber color as Megan's had been.

Chapter Five

The low rumble of conversation punctuated by clinking crystal, classical music and occasional high-pitched laughter spilled out of the massive double doors as the Trent entered the mansion. A tray of champagne in flutes floated past and he took a glass, raising it at a pretty brunette before taking a small sip. He hated champagne. Vile, metallic-tasting stuff, but it gave the appearance of normalcy. Moving closer to the brunette, he took stock of her body, his gaze starting at her shoulder-length wavy hair and traveling down over her shoulders, her breasts, her hips, her legs, and finally...no. He turned away, the bite of champagne on his tongue no match for the horror he'd just seen. It was going to be a long night.

He circulated through the crowd, greeting people he knew, shaking hands with those he didn't, playing the bored rich bachelor everyone expected. It was taxing, and within the first hour and a half, he was ready to make his excuses. Confronted with a dearth of strappy sandals, peep-toe pumps and even the occasional pair of flip-flops, he'd seen more dry skin, faded tattoos and mangled toenails than he ever wanted to again, and while there were a few possibilities, none perfect enough for his Angel.

Setting his unfinished drink down, he made his way through the people to the parlor where he'd last seen his brother. As expected, he was still ensconced in a high-backed wing chair, surrounded by his adoring fans as cigar smoke coated the room in a swirling, noxious haze. Todd Abernathy was running for congressional office, and these fundraisers were a monthly excuse to drink, smoke and con people out of yet more money for a campaign he was fully capable of funding himself. Trent didn't see the point of involving others, but then he never had. Stifling a cough, he approached his brother, anxious to take his leave and escape the circus-like atmosphere.

"Trent!" Todd called, spotting him. "Just the man I wanted to see. There's someone I want you to meet."

Fighting the urge to roll his eyes, he forced his lips into a pleasant smile and wished he had another drink. "Good news for me," he said, noting two women at Todd's side as he drew closer. He nodded at Jackie, Todd's blond trophy-wife. Not very smart, but gorgeous, and he noted that her feet were impeccable, of course. Too bad she was off limits. She smiled back, raising one hand for a tiny finger-wave before letting it fall to rest on Todd's shoulder. He stopped in front of Todd, his attention drawn to the woman standing beside Jackie. Tall and slender with her own blond hair swept up in a sophisticated style, her brown eyes sparkled with intelligence. He held out his hand, his heart rate picking up as she took it, her grip firm and confident.

"Alice Burton," she said, her voice melodic. Perhaps even angelic.

He released her reluctantly. "It's very nice to meet you, Alice. What brings a high-class girl like yourself to a party like this?" He took in the sparkling green sheath hugging her curves, the tan-but-not-orange skin, and finally her feet, resting on clear glass-looking pumps with geometric cut-outs along the sides. Smooth skin unmarred by purple veins, straight, naturally pleasing shape, and perfectly manicured pale pink toenails all equaled absolute perfection. He looked into her knowing eyes.

"One could ask the same of you, Mr. Abernathy - I've heard you don't particularly care for these events either. Though you certainly seem to be in your element at the moment."

He laughed. "Indeed I am," he said, stepping a little closer, forcing her to tilt her head back in order to maintain eye contact. "I've been looking for something, you see. And I think I may have just found it."

* * *

Jake sipped a Styrofoam cup of strong, thick coffee the next morning as he waited for Agent Paige to return to her desk. It had taken a long time to calm Megan down last night, but he'd finally been able to go home and sleep. Not that it had helped. He'd dreamed of angels with red, open eye sockets, and woke up reaching for his face to make sure his own eyes hadn't disappeared.

He checked his watch, eight forty-five. Maybe she'd been called out on a case. He considered what her life must be like, always on call, always having to be ready to go at a moment's notice. Occasionally a patient would need something after hours, but he considered himself lucky that it didn't happen more often. And when it did, it was pretty rare to encounter a dead body.

Strong, confident footsteps clicked down the hall, and his pulse jumped as he recognized her gait. He leaned forward, willing his body to behave. She was as hard as they came, but he wouldn't be much of a man if he didn't appreciate her assets, so to speak. *Look where that got you last time*, he thought, his excitement doused at the thought of Redding.

"Good morning, Werner. I see you found the coffee."

He nodded. "Jake. And I think I've discovered why

51

you don't drink it," he said, indicating the designer cup in her hand. "Smart woman."

She set her things on the desk, removing the dark sunglasses to reveal tired eyes. Apparently he wasn't the only one who'd had trouble sleeping last night. "So," she said, settling in her chair. "How's Ms. Hunter?"

"She finally calmed down. I went home a little after midnight. Any more clues as to where those eyes came from?"

She rifled through a short stack of papers, passing one to him across the desk. "Turns out they're prosthetics," she said, folding her hands on the desk. "There's a chip embedded in each, and some connections on the back that our lab rats seem to think are meant to hook up to the optical nerve."

He raised his eyebrows. "So she could see again? Does that really work?"

Paige shrugged. "Hard to say. It's possible, but since there's no evidence of this ever being used on anyone, it appears to be a prototype." She took the report back and placed it on the pile. "The more important question is, why? Why would someone steal her eyes, try to kill her, and then send her a new pair of eyes? It doesn't make sense."

Jake shook his head. "Guilt, maybe." He closed his eyes, trying to put himself in the killer's mind. He'd cleaned everything spotless, drugged his victim before he grabbed her, stripped her clothing, lay her in the bathtub...the only thing that he hadn't meant to do was let her live.

"It's mercy," he said, opening his eyes and leaning forward. Paige frowned, but waited for him to continue. "He feels bad that he left her alive. He never meant to let her live without sight. I'd bet anything that he's trying to help."

It was Agent Paige's turn to shake her head. "That doesn't make any sense - why not just finish the job later?"

"Because he can't."

* * *

"He can't?" Agent Paige's expression was one of disbelief. "The man's killed several women now, and you're telling me he has some sort of moral code that will keep him from targeting Ms. Hunter twice?"

Jake didn't blame her being skeptical. "That's exactly what I'm saying. Look on the bright side though. That same code keeps him from killing just anyone, and it will probably be what allows us to find him. It also makes it unlikely he's a psychopath, which works to our advantage as well."

Paige nodded slowly. "I'm not sure I buy that, but we'll go with it for now since it's about all we've got." She took a sip of coffee then turned her computer monitor so he could see. "I went through the security tapes the other night, and I've got a few possibilities. The only problem is, the cameras are positioned to face the cash registers rather than the customers, so we don't have any good facial shots to go on." Four pictures appeared onscreen, Different men who'd gone through Megan's line in the past two weeks. Two were in business dress, one in casual clothing and one in a bulky winter coat that hid his fashion choices.

"What made you pick these four?" Jake asked, peering at the photos. He examined Megan's expression, and the set of each subject's shoulders. Nothing jumped out to say any of them were the killer.

Megan shrugged. "These four were the only men who came in alone. There's a camera out front that we used the tapes from to determine single shoppers. She also looked at each of them directly, so they're most likely to have seen her eyes."

"What makes you so sure he'd be alone?"

Paige sat back in her chair, rubbing her head with one hand. "Why would someone who kills women for their eyes have friends?"

Jake chuckled. "I doubt his hobby comes up in conversation," he said gently. "There's no reason a serial killer who isn't a sociopath wouldn't be able to have relatively normal relationships. This guy is organized, neat, and clearly plans his attacks out very thoroughly. A sociopath is often disorganized, erratic and probably would have left some clue by accident. We're either looking for a psychopath or a very organized, focused individual with a very specific reason for killing those women. Either of those personality types would be capable of having normal, or normal-looking relationships."

"Okay. So how do you suggest we find this guy then?"

He thought for a moment. "We need to go through the files again, and look for any inconsistency, no matter how small. We know he has boundaries, and we need to figure out what those are to narrow down the potential victims."

Paige nodded. "Maybe we missed something in the interviews too." She thought for a moment, frowning. "Why just the eyes? He doesn't do anything else to these women, very deliberately. What use would he have for a bunch of eyeballs?"

"Could be a lot of things," Jake said, finishing off his coffee. "Maybe some sort of religious thing. But just to be thorough, has anyone checked for similar crimes with different body parts?"

She picked up the phone and dialed a number. "John I need you to do a search for any dismemberment cases for the past six months. Bring the files to my office when you're done? Thanks." She hung up and stood, gathering up her tablet and the coffee. "Come on, Dr. Werner. Let's dig through the files we have again."

* * *

Jake tossed his keys on the counter, switching on the kitchen light. He rubbed a hand over his face and through his hair, inhaling deep, then letting it out slow. The microwave clock read eleven-thirty, and all he wanted was to fall into bed. He'd spent most of the day going over files with Agent Paige, and while there wasn't anything concrete yet, he was starting to get a feel for the killer. The personality certainly seemed to match Trent Abernathy, though they hadn't found any real evidence that would match him to the victims. He grabbed a beer out of the fridge and kicked off his shoes, padding into the living room to sprawl out on the couch.

Just as he pointed the remote at the TV, someone knocked hard on the front door. Exactly twice.

He left the hall light off as he approached, peering cautiously through the window. The stoop was empty, save a thin envelope on the welcome mat. Slowly pulling the door in, he squatted down, careful to glance around the front yard even as he reached for the package. Only after he'd locked himself inside did he let out the breath he hadn't realized he was holding.

The envelope was thin, and he recognized the file inside as the final Abernathy file that had gone missing at the office last night. On the cover was a sticky note that read, "Meet me at 722 Ricochet Drive, midnight. You need to see this. Angela"

He checked his watch. Ten minutes wasn't enough

time to get across town, but he had to try. If nothing else, he wanted to know why Redding had stolen the file, and then returned it. He ran to the kitchen and put on his shoes then grabbed the keys and hurried to the garage. With any luck, she'd wait.

It was ten after when he pulled to the curb across the street from the house. A modern mansion, it was set back on the property, an imposing shadow over-looking a massive estate, surrounded by a ten-foot iron fence on all sides. Whoever lived here was serious about privacy and money.

He reached for the door latch just as the passenger door opened and Angela Redding slid into the seat next to him. "Don't get out," she said, her voice low and raspy. "Just wait. They should be back soon." Her eyes were bright with excitement, though he clearly saw fear lurking in the depths as well.

"Who is 'they'?" he asked, glancing back at the house again. "Why are we here?"

She hunched over, tugging at his sleeve. "Scoot down so they don't see you. If he's on time..." She glanced over the back seat, then tugged at him again. "They're coming. Just watch."

Jake slid down until his eyes were even with the base of the window. Angela looked over his shoulder as he watched, her breath warm on his face. A tall man came into view, slender, an old-fashioned white fedora covering his head. His suit was light as well, re-flecting moonlight as he strolled beside a woman nearly as tall in high spike-heels and a short dress. A long, twisted wood cane in the man's hand appeared to be just for show.

"He has those suits specially made," Angela whispered. "They're bamboo. He wears them a few times then composts them in his back yard."

Jake hid his surprise, suppressing the urge to look at her as he watched the man enter a code to the front gate. "How would you know that?" he asked as the couple walked up the drive. "And why?"

"Sssh..." she laid a hand on his arm, her fingers tightening. "Keep watching. Any minute now..."

The gate swung closed, and a few seconds later, the man with the cane bent down and scooped the woman beside him into his arms.

Angela's breath hitched in his ear. "Do you see? He's got her now. She won't come back out."

"Just because he picked her up doesn't mean--"

"Look at her head."

Jake reached behind him and got a digital camera out of the center console. He turned it on and pointed it toward the couple, zooming in on the man's back. The woman was clearly unconscious; her head lolling back over his arm at an odd angle.

Chapter Six

Trent sat in the library, slowly swirling his brandy as he looked thoughtfully at Angel. He'd secured Alice Burton in one of the guest rooms to await surgery, but it felt wrong. Not in a moral sense, but rather in the sense that he'd missed something. He shifted uneasily.

"We have a problem, darling," he said, leaning forward to brace his elbows on his knees. "I've found a perfect pair of feet for you. Unfortunately, I think we may have to pass due to issues with the donor. At least for tonight."

Angel's breath fogged the glass lightly as her chest moved in and out. The bright, hazel eyes looked sagely down at him, calm. Reassuring. Just as he'd hoped.

"Ah, Angel. I knew you'd understand. It shouldn't be long, I don't think. But I'm afraid if we rush things, it could have...detrimental consequences for us both." He sat back and sipped his drink, glancing at the clock on the wall. Nearly one in the morning. The drugs he'd given her would wear off in half-an-hour or so, and the explanation would be more plausible if he was there when she woke.

He finished his drink and set the glass deliberately on the side table. Rising, he approached the glass and traced the shape of her face with one finger. "You know what may have to be done, darling. But you have my heart. Always." He leaned forward and pressed his lips to the case then hid his creation. Turning off the lights, he walked quickly upstairs to the guest wing, unbuttoning his shirt as he went.

Ms. Burton was still sleeping when he unlocked the door and entered her room. With smooth, silent movements he released the soft lined cuffs anchoring her wrists and ankles to the bed, pushing them out of sight. He'd removed her clothing earlier, and he scattered the items on the floor along with his own, gritting his teeth until the urge to pick them up had passed. Sliding beneath the covers, he pulled her back flush with his front, spooning her unconscious body. Closing his eyes, he let out a long breath, slowing his heart rate even as she began to stir. Just in time, it seemed.

"Trent?" she whispered, turning in his arms.

He opened his eyes a little, giving her a lazy smile. "Welcome back. I'm afraid you passed out for a bit, my dear." Pressing a gentle kiss to her lips, he cupped the side of her face with his hand, imagining it was

Angel he caressed. "Feeling better?"

She rolled to her back, running a hand over her forehead. "I have a horrible headache, actually." Turning her head to look at him, she frowned. "I don't remember anything after we went for that walk..."

Trent tried to look wounded. "Oh, now that hurts. You don't remember coming in and having a drink - or three - with me?"

"I'm sorry." She shook her head, then groaned before continuing. "Obviously we had a good time. I normally don't do this - pass out on my dates, I mean."

He slowly ran his fingers up and down her neck, then sideways over her collarbone. "No worries, love. I'm sorry you don't remember. Would you like me to take you home now, so you can recover?" *Please say yes.*

She turned on her side again, facing him, and ran her fingers lightly over his chest, tracing his ribs and moving lower. Her lips found his neck. Kissed him.

Damn.

He hated this part.

* * *

"We need to call someone," Jake said, his elbow contacting something soft as he dug in his pocket for his cell phone. He scrolled through numbers, bringing up the last call he got from Agent Paige.

Angela grabbed his arm. "No," she hissed, still watching the driveway. "I've tried before, the police won't do anything. No evidence, they say."

He took the phone with his other hand and pressed send. "We're not calling the police. I'm working with the FBI on another project. The agent I'm working with might be interested in taking a look."

Angela sat back in her seat, silent as he waited for Paige to pick up. He wasn't surprised when she didn't sound the least bit groggy. He explained the situation and hung up when she agreed to join them. Looking over at his companion, he met an intense stare that made him want to squirm in his seat. It was obvious she had something on her mind, the way she kept biting her lip and curling her fingers into the seat. Knowing he'd regret it, he gave in to curiosity.

"Something on your mind?"

She looked down at her hands. "What made you decide to look at his files?"

"You know I can't discuss--"

"That's crap, and you know it." She shook her head. "I saw the file, Dr. Werner. I know what Trent told you...about me. How can you protect him when you know what he did? What kind of a monster he is?"

Jake ran a hand over his head, breathing deep. "There's no evidence that anything happened, Angela. Even if I wasn't bound by the client/patient relationship, I can't just go accusing people of things they may or may not have done."

"But I know--"

"No, you *think*." He held a hand up when she would have spoken. "Do you have any evidence? Anything that proves he took you or anyone else?"

"I've seen what we just watched several times - isn't that enough? Those women, they go in, and they never come back out. He doesn't bury them. He doesn't throw them out with the trash. As far as I can tell, he waits until the wee hours of the morning and takes them somewhere, but I've never managed to follow him. I always get lost."

"That's probably just as well," Jake muttered, jumping at a strong tap on the glass. He unlocked the back door, and Agent Paige slid in behind him.

"Angela Redding, Agent Kate Paige. Why don't you tell her what you think is going on?"

As Angela told her story, Jake watched the big house. He scanned the area through the camera lens, silently berating himself for not clicking the shutter in the few short seconds he'd had the woman in his sights. Everything was dark, quiet, and had he just been walking by, he would've assumed the old mansion was deserted, even though the grounds and residence were both well-manicured.

Using the zoom function, he examined each window closely in turn, imagining what might be beyond the curtains. An old parlor, antique furniture, maybe a

63

dusty library. Or perhaps the owner had more con-temporary tastes. He panned to the upper left win-dow, and froze, his heart racing in his chest. Trent Abernathy stood just behind the glass, staring right into the camera with and intense, predatory glare.

"He knows we're here." Jake lowered the camera, still unable to look away from the window. "And I don't think he's all that happy about it." The car shif-ted as both women leaned over to look at the house, Agent Paige in the back seat and Angela over his shoulder. He handed Paige the camera "Upper left window."

"I see him," she said. "Unless he's picking up a re-flection off the lens, he can't see us though. Maybe the moon is bright enough, but I doubt it."

Angela moved back to the passenger seat. "No, he knows. Somehow, he always knows when I'm out here, watching. Sometimes he waves, sometimes he just watches back. I think he likes it in some sick way."

Jake turned, noting the weariness in her voice. "How often do you watch him?"

"A couple nights a week. He goes out late a night, and sometimes doesn't come back until just before dawn. I'd think he was a vampire if I believed they ex-ist."

"The women - they never come back out while you're watching?" Paige asked. Jake looked over the seat at her, making notes on her computer. Angela shifted, turning so she could look back as well.

"No, they never come out at all," she said, her tone firm. "When he brings one home, which is rare, I wait. Sometimes well into the next day. They don't ever come out."

Paige sighed, looking up at Angela with a mixture of pity and understanding. "But you can't be here all the time. And without a body or some other proof..."

Angela shook her head. "The next night he drives them somewhere...but they're in the trunk of his car. I see him getting things ready, putting plastic in his trunk, backing the car up to the house, carrying something out. Something body-sized. I *know*."

Jake reached out to take one of Angela's trembling hands. "Okay," he said, shooting a warning look at Paige. Angela was on the edge, and the last thing they needed was a nervous breakdown just now. "Maybe we should call it a night then. We can come back tomorrow night and wait for him to move her. Would that be okay?"

"He won't do it." She pulled her hand away, looking at something over his shoulder. "He knows there are more people now, he probably even knows who you are. He isn't stupid enough to move the body when he knows there will be more witnesses."

Jake glanced over his shoulder at the big house. "You might be right. Then again, if our presence changed his routine, maybe there won't be a body. This might be too much of a risk for him."

Paige leaned forward, frowning. "Did you recognize any of the women, Angela? Was there anything similar about them - hair, eyes, build - anything at all?"

Angela thought for a moment. "They're always tall and slender, with long hair. I'm never really close enough to see anything more." Her brows drew together as she looked over Jake's shoulder again. "Just like that." She pointed, and Jake turned, hearing Paige scoot over to the window again as well. Walking unsteadily down the drive was the woman Abernathy had carried inside over an hour before, long blond hair shimmering in the moonlight.

Alive and alone.

"Should we question her?" Jake asked, every muscle in his body shouting to at least go help the woman to her car. She was weaving on her heels, her ankles crossing at every third step.

"We can't," Paige replied from the back seat. "We don't have any grounds - she came of her own accord, and no one's stopping her from leaving. We don't have any evidence against Abernathy, so technically there's nothing to question her about."

Angela sighed. "Right. Technically nothing happened tonight. Even though the poor woman can hardly stand on her own." She reached for the door handle. "We can't question her, but I think it's pretty clear she needs a doctor. I'm going to see if she wants a ride."

The woman stopped at the gate briefly, leaning heavily on the iron railing and looking back at the house. The gate began to swing open and she stumbled back, then forward through the fissure and down the drive to the sidewalk. Jake watched Angela jog across the street and take the woman's hand, talking to her for a moment before leading her carefully back to the car.

"I'd better not be involved in this, in case it eventually crosses my desk in an official capacity," Paige said, sliding across the seat to the other side of the car. "See you tomorrow?"

"Sure. I'll be there."

She opened the door and got out, closing it just as Angela opened the other door for Abernathy's date. Jake glanced over the seat as the woman settled into the car with a dreamy smile. "You're cute," she said, leaning forward to trace a pattern on his upper arm as Angela closed the door. "Are you the driver?"

Jake grinned. "I am tonight, ma'am. What's your name?" Angela got in beside him, and shot him a disapproving look.

"Alice Burton," the woman said in a sing-song voice. "Where are you taking me?"

He looked at Angela, who subtly shook her head. Turning back to Alice, he winked. "It's a surprise. Do you like surprises?"

She sat back, her brows furrowed as she considered the question. "I don't think so," she said finally, pausing to nibble her lower lip. "But I'll make an exception because you're so cute. Even if you do have a girlfriend." Looking pointedly at Angela, she crossed her arms over her chest and stuck her bottom lip out in a dramatic pout.

He chuckled, turning in the driver's seat to start the car. "I appreciate that, Alice. We'll be there soon, I promise." He pulled away from the curb, trying not to flinch at the fingertips tickling his neck.

Fifteen minutes later, he pulled up to the emergency room entrance. "Is she still asleep?" he whispered, turning off the ignition.

Angela nodded. "I'll go get someone." She opened the door as quietly as possible, and left it ajar as she jogged through the double sliding doors. Not long after she as back with two attendants and a gurney. Alice didn't wake up even when they lifted her out of the car. A bad sign, Jake thought as he watched them wheel her away. Alice got back in the car and exhaled slowly.

"So now what?" he asked.

She shrugged. "They won't have any results for a few hours. I told them I'm her sister, which will work until she wakes up, but who knows if they'll call or not. I guess you can go home and get some sleep."

He drove out of the parking lot, back toward Abernathy's house and his car. "What about you?"

"I'll come back and sit with her until she's awake, if they'll let me."

Chapter Seven

From a darkened window, Trent stood in his lounge pants and watched Dr. Werner and Angela drive off with Alice. He'd made the right decision, sending her out to them, but it was still rather disappointing to have missed out on such a lovely pair of feet. *Ah well. Next time.*

Still, she would need to be taken care of. He couldn't afford to leave loose ends lying around any longer, and who knows what she might remember.

Just about to turn away, movement from the corner by the garage caught his eye. He frowned. The security system was armed and the gate was closed. No one should have been able to get onto the property. He waited, straining to see into the shadows, but there was nothing. Had he imagined it?

Reaching for a shirt, he pulled it over his head, walking quickly to his large master closet and stepped inside, activating a hidden latch on the back wall. A portion of the wall swung away and he entered the panic room, pressing the portal closed behind him. The room was gray, all concrete and steel, with a long shiny metal counter running the length of one wall. Several screens were mounted right into the wall above, and he sat in a leather executive's chair, pulling a keyboard and mouse forward on the counter.

A few keystrokes brought up the garage and surrounding area, shrouded in darkness. He rewound the recording five minutes, turned on the infrared filter and hit play. Sure enough, a small figure crept hunched over between the garage and the fence, freezing in place as soon as it had reached the driveway. His lips turned up. Perhaps a game of cat and mouse was just what he needed to salvage the evening.

Going back to the live feed, he turned on the infrared filter, but the figure was no longer there. He set the system to scan, impatiently tapping his fingers against the cold metal as he waited for each camera to update the live feed. Images scrolled by like a movie on fast forward, until a red blob flashed into view. The scan stopped, and he used the mouse to zoom in, then turned off the infrared.

He grinned.

Well, well. He rocked back in his chair as a petite woman with straight blond hair crossed the back yard and ducked into the shed he kept his gardening equipment in. "My apologies Agent Paige, but I'm afraid there's nothing in there you'd be interested in my dear," he said as she came out three minutes later. "You really don't think I'm that stupid, do you?"

She sprinted toward the house, the motion-activated cameras following. As she approached the back door, Trent thought for a moment, considering his options. Angel would kill, so to speak, for that lovely blond hair. Unfortunately too many people knew Agent Paige was interested in him, so making her disappear wasn't an option. Yet.

But that didn't mean he couldn't have a little fun, did it? After all, she was on private property. Without a warrant. Or backup. She was kneeling in front of the door, her hands busy at the lock. He watched for a few minutes, until she sat back on her heels, frustrated. Nice to have someone aside from himself confirm the company's pick-proof claims.

"Come on, darling. Just one more time," he coaxed, moving the mouse over a green button at the top of the screen. "I'll even help this time."

She leaned forward and inserted something into the keyhole, her motions deliberate. Trent clicked the button, enjoying the confusion on her face when the door swung in a couple inches. She stood, slowly pushing it open just enough to slip inside. It shut behind her, and Trent slid the keyboard and mouse back to their proper places. Exiting through the closet back into his bedroom, he smiled, anticipation sending delicious chills up the back of his neck.

* * *

Jake dropped Angela off at her car a few houses over from Abernathy's estate. After her taillights disappeared down the street, he drove around the block to slowly cruise past the mansion one more time. Expecting the same darkened facade as before, he frowned as a bright yellow light suddenly flickered on in one of the lower front windows. More interesting though was the female shape silhouetted behind the nearly-sheer curtains. He pulled over and watched, wondering if the other woman had been there all along, or if she'd come by later. Was Abernathy seeing two women at once?

The woman in profile shifted, the movement vaguely familiar. He watched another figure approach her from behind, and grabbed the camera, zooming the lens in on the window. The features were still muted, but he could make out straight, sleek hair, a slender frame and that excellent posture that was intimidating as hell. It had to be Kate Paige, though what she was doing in Abernathy's house was...

He swung the camera to focus on the man creeping up behind her. His heart pounded as a hand came up, holding something long and pointed out to the side, headed straight for Paige.

Jake grabbed his phone and dialed her number. She

didn't move to answer the call. Why not? He tossed the phone on the other seat, trying to think of something else that would interrupt the scene playing out before his eyes. He held his arm over the steering wheel, hesitating a moment too long. The man's arm wrapped around Paige's neck and engulfed her as Jake watched, focusing the camera on the window again with shaking hands. Paige slumped over and Abernathy let her slide to the floor, standing over her for a minute longer. Then he walked away, and a few seconds later, the window went dark.

Jake lay down across the seats, hoping Abernathy couldn't see him. What had he done to Paige, and why had he turned the light on in the first place - wouldn't it have been easier to sneak up on her in the dark? And what had she been thinking, going in there by herself? He considered his options, then stowed both the phone and the camera in his pockets. He could call the FBI, but then Abernathy would know they were watching him. Not to mention the trouble Kate would be in if they found out about this. There was only one thing to do. He'd have to go in there and bring her out.

This is a bad idea, he thought as he scooted across the seat to the passenger door and let himself out, closing the door quietly behind him. *Abernathy's going to kill us and dump us out in the desert somewhere.* He used the neighbor's bushes for cover, working his way down the street until his position wasn't visible from any windows in Abernathy's house. Jogging across the street, he pushed between the fence and a wall of lilacs, then pulled himself over the estate wall. Landing just behind the garage, he crouched down, making his way as quickly as he dared toward the house.

Jake flattened himself against the dark corner of the mansion, keeping still as he willed his heart rate back down to a normal level. Abernathy was smart. He probably had the whole place under surveillance and Jake knew his presence wouldn't be a secret for long. Careful to stay in the deepest shadow, he moved slowly along the side of the house, tugging gently at each basement window as he passed, but they were all locked. As he approached the back corner of the house, he nearly tripped on a pair of narrow wooden doors slanting up from the ground. The cellar - perfect.

Running a hand over the top, he found the handle and pulled, but the door wouldn't budge. The back of his knuckles brushed against small plastic squares under the knob, and he bent close, straining to make out the digits on a number pad. Setting aside his curiosity at why anyone would put a digital lock on a cellar, he thought for a moment, trying to figure out what the code might be. Would a wrong code set off an alarm?

He took his cell phone out of his pocket and shielded the light with his hand as he looked at the number pad. Then he reached out with a surprisingly steady finger to key in five digits on the door lock: 2-

6-4-3-5.

The letters above those numbers on the keypad spelled a-n-g-e-l.

The click of the lock disengaging sounded like a gunshot in the still night air. Relieved that no alarms seemed to be going off, he pulled the door up and used the light from his phone to start down the steep wooden stairs. As the door settled back into place, another loud snap engaged the lock with a startling finality.

He reached the bottom, confused at the hard cement floor beneath his feet rather than the expected packed earth. The air was fresh and clean, and even in the darkness the room felt open rather than stifling. The light from his phone wasn't much help - it was enough to illuminate the floor ahead, but didn't reach far enough to reveal anything else. He moved forward, swinging the light side to side and going slow to avoid a collision with any objects that might be waiting in the dark.

Finally reaching a wooden door, he felt the wall to the side and found a light switch. Hesitating a moment, his curiosity won and he pushed it up, illuminating the room in a cool florescent white glow. Putting his phone away, he blinked several times, waiting for his eyes to adjust to the brightness before he turned around.

When he finally did, he wished he hadn't.

The room was large, fitting his original impression.

Metal shelves much like the ones in his file room lined two of the walls, holding boxes, bags and jars holding small body parts suspended in fluid. One jar in particular stood out, a large gallon pickle-jar filled with eyeballs all seemingly staring at him. He could barely tear his gaze away to examine the rest of the room.

At the back of the room a wide metal table sat beneath a collection of shiny, well-kept tools. Under the table were buckets and other assorted items, all lined up just so. A metal lamp hanging above illuminated the center of the table with an eerie red light.

There was another door near the table, and Jake knew for certain he didn't want to know where it led. Panic collected in his stomach, and he turned off the light, plunging the room into darkness as he pulled the door beside him open. He wasn't sure how, but he needed to get to Paige as soon as possible.

Stepping out into the main basement, Jake closed the door to the cellar room, careful to minimize the noise. The complete darkness left him no choice but to use his phone for light again, and he moved as quietly as he could through the rooms until he found a wooden staircase. Keeping to the edge, he went up, stepping light to avoid whatever creaks the old risers might have. When he reached the top, he put his phone away, swallowing hard. If Abernathy was on the other side of the door, that would be it.

For several moments he stood there, breathing

softly and listening for any movement on the other side. Finally he pushed the door open just an inch, and peered out, noting the back door was only five steps away. Emboldened by the information, he slipped out into the hallway, easing the door closed behind him. Peering around the corners on either side of the stairwell, he decided to take his chances with the kitchen. The living room hadn't worked out well for Paige this evening, and he hoped there was a back staircase to the upper floors that the staff used. If Paige was unconscious, she was probably in a room upstairs somewhere - or that would make the most logical sense, to make her easy for Abernathy to deal with.

However he dealt with interlopers.

As Jake moved down the hall toward the kitchen, his pulse beat faster. Glasses clinked together and a cork popped as someone moved around the kitchen. Dim light spilled out over the threshold, perhaps from an oven hood or the refrigerator. Drinks? He frowned. Maybe he'd misjudged the situation. Even so, Paige needed to know what kind of trouble she was in.

He ducked into the dining room and found a dark corner where he was hidden, but could still see the kitchen door. It seemed like hours before the light finally flicked off and he tensed, pressing back against the wall to avoid being seen. But the footsteps faded in the opposite direction. He waited until he couldn't hear them any longer, and then slowly left his position to explore the kitchen. Through the door on the other end, he entered another hall, with a staircase to his left. The servant's, no doubt. He made his way up the stairs and onto the second floor. There was a light coming out of a wide doorway down the hall and he went toward it, thankful for the carpeting that muffled his steps. Flattening his back to the wall just outside the open French doors, he started to peer around the corner.

"Join us, Dr. Werner. I've been expecting you."

Jake nearly bolted at Abernathy's words. Even though he'd suspected that his presence wasn't a secret, it was still unsettling to be addressed directly. He moved into the doorway, struck by two things at once that rendered him speechless.

Abernathy was seated in a large leather armchair with his back to the door. On a couch beside him, Agent Paige sat quietly with her legs crossed, dressed in only a nude colored bra and judging from the strip of lavender curving around her hip, a pair of silky panties. She didn't look up as he moved forward, just sipped from the glass of wine in one hand and stared straight ahead.

On the back wall, a large glass case was illuminated with a yellowish light, and inside a woman seemed to float as she looked out. He went closer, until he was standing right in front of her, and struggled for words as he stared into her eyes. Megan's eyes? He looked at

Abernathy in disbelief.

"Her eyes," Jake said, pointing to the glass case. "Those are...but they can't be..."

Abernathy smiled, something between sympathy and amusement on his face. "Beautiful, isn't she? Come, sit down and have some wine. It will help ease the shock."

Chapter Eight

Smiling, Trent handed Dr. Werner a glass of wine as he sank slowly to the couch opposite Agent Paige. The man looked a bit shocked as his focus switched from Angel to the nearly-naked woman across from him. Sitting back in his chair, Trent watched as the psychologist tried to come to terms with what he was seeing.

"Kate? Are you okay? Where are your clothes?"

The FBI agent took another sip of wine, her glassy eyes looking briefly at Trent before turning back to Werner. "I'm fine," she said, her voice soft and breathy. "I was hot."

Werner took a healthy gulp of wine, then another. Good.

"It's such a pleasure to have you both here this evening," Trent said, nodding at his companions. "It's rare that Angel and I have visitors. To what do I owe the honor?"

Werner shook his head, his brows drawing together. "We...ah, were just in the neighborhood..."

Trent laughed. "Oh come now, Dr. Werner. Is that the best you can do?"

"Agent Paige and I were looking for a woman - one you might know. I can't remember..." He shook his head again, setting the glass on the coffee table. "My head." He rubbed his temples with his hands, then picked up the glass again, sniffing near the opening.

Smart man, Trent thought as he watched Werner wrinkle his nose.

"There's something in the wine," Werner said, setting the glass down again and looking up. "What did you do to us?"

Trent shrugged, talking a sip from his own glass. "It's just a little something to help you forget," he said, noting that Werner's eyes were starting to glaze as well. It wouldn't be long now.

Werner pulled at the collar of his shirt. "It's hot in here," he said, squirming in his seat. "Can you turn the air conditioning on?"

"I'm afraid not. But feel free to remove your clothing if you wish. We're all friends here." *And it will make things easier later.*

Werner pulled his shirt over his head, breathing a sigh of relief. It was impressive how fast the new drug was working, even on a man of his size. It was just a side experiment, a hobby, really, but Trent was pleased to have found such responsive volunteers. Just a few more tests.

"Dr. Werner," he said, waiting for the man to look at him. It was clear from his slow movements that the drug was nearly at full effect. "I think you should apologize to Angel for staring at her earlier tonight. It was rude."

Werner stood up, slowly, and walked to stand in front of the display case. "I'm sorry I stared," he said, each word enunciated slowly and deliberately, as if he was having trouble with his tongue. "It was rude, and I apologize."

"Very good," Trent said. "Now come back and sit down, please."

Werner returned to his seat, and Trent turned to Agent Paige. "Tell me, agent - what were you doing before you came to my house?"

"I'm not...um..." she frowned, then shrugged. "I don't remember."

"What's the last thing you do remember?" He sat forward. This would tell him just how retroactive the drug was, which was of vital importance.

Again, she hesitated. "I got home from work, and ate dinner...and then I was here."

Trent turned to Werner. "What's the last thing you remember, doctor?"

"I got in the car to meet someone..." he paused. "I must have come here after that? I don't remember anything else..."

"Very good." Trent sat back, trying to contain his excitement. "Please, enjoy the rest of your wine, both of you. Then I'll make sure you get home."

* * *

Pain lanced sharply through Jake's brain as he rolled to his back. Pressing a hand to each side of his head, he groaned, nausea seizing his stomach muscles with a savage intensity. His legs instinctively curled up and he rolled again, coming to rest against a solid object. Then the object groaned too, and he pried one eye open just enough to see long blond hair and a slender, naked back trembling violently. Falling onto his back again, he waited for the spasms to abate, then swallowed in an attempt to moisten his cottony mouth.

"What the hell happened?" he croaked, wincing at the sound of his own too-loud voice. The mattress dipped beside him, and he carefully turned his head to the side as the woman slowly sat up. Still trembling she doubled over, holding her stomach. Jake watched, powerless to help her as recognition slowly came into focus. "Kate?"

The shaking subsided, and she looked over her shoulder, moving carefully. "You're sick too." It wasn't a question, but he nodded anyway, the motion sending another round of electric sparks through his head. "Then you didn't poison me," she said, her voice like needles in his skin. Probably hers too, he allowed as he tried to will the pain away.

"Maybe we should call someone," he whispered, rolling away from her as fresh spasms attacked. "I don't remember anything, do you?"

He waited a long time for an answer, finally forcing himself to twist back the other way. She'd disappeared, and he crawled to the edge of the bed, but didn't see her on the floor. Completely spent by the effort, he closed his eyes. He'd get up in just a minute and go find her. She couldn't have gotten far in their condition.

A few minutes later, someone was shaking his shoulder. "Jake, wake up. Hey, are you okay?"

He opened his eyes, relieved to see Angela's concerned face. Moving cautiously, he lifted his head. The dull throbbing between his temples was nothing like the pain in his dream, thank god. Sitting up, he leaned back against the headboard and breathed in deep, his stomach muscles protesting the effort. "I had the worst dream," he said, rubbing his face with his hands. "I thought I was dying, and Kate was here...damn. More like a nightmare, I guess." Dropping his hands to his lap, he frowned at the odd expression on Angela's face as she sat beside him. "Why are you here, anyway? How did you get in?"

"The door was open." She glanced away for a moment, then looked down at the bed. "Do you remember anything about last night?"

He thought back, the dream with Agent Paige still fresh in his mind, but before that, it was like a white wall. He closed his eyes, going back to when he'd left the FBI office. "I came home, got something to eat...I remember opening an envelope?"

Angela nodded. "The one I left for you, asking you to meet me outside Abernathy's house. Do you remember what we saw?"

He shook his head, the thrumming in his head worse. "I don't remember anything about last night. Nothing after the envelope. And then the dream this morning."

"Um, about that." She put a hand on his arm, and squeezed gently. "I don't think it was a dream, Jake. When I came in, I found that FBI agent sprawled naked on the floor in the hall. I woke her up, and she said the same thing you did - she can't remember anything from last night. I think you were both drugged."

"Kate--uh, Agent Paige is here?" Jake sat up straight, looking around the room. "Where is she?"

Angela nodded toward the door. "She's taking a shower in the bathroom down the hall. She was pretty confused when I woke her up. I told her I'd wake you, and then we'd talk when you were both up and ready. Do you want some coffee?"

"I think that would be a good idea."

She squeezed his hand and stood, hesitating for a moment before she left the room. He swung his legs over the side of the bed, relieved when there were no ill effects from the movement. When he stood, the room spun, but it was over quickly and he found he could walk without too much trouble. The low throbbing in his head reminded him of...something, though he couldn't quite say what. A shower could definitely help. He went to the master bathroom and turned on the water, chasing an image of a naked and soapy Kate from his mind as fast as it came in. Apparently his libido hadn't been affected. He grinned at the thought.

Stepping under the warm spray, he tried again to remember what had happened when he left the house the night before. The information was there, he could feel it locked away, but no matter what he tried it was impossible to access. By the time he toweled off he'd only succeeded in making his headache worse, and increasing the frustration of not knowing. Dressing quickly, he went to the kitchen, the need to know what Angela could tell him at critical levels.

She and Paige were sitting on stools at the counter, sipping coffee in silence. They both looked up as he walked in, and Angela pushed a third cup toward him as he took a seat.

"Feel better?" she asked.

He nodded as the warm liquid slid down his throat, then looked at Paige. She avoided his gaze. "A little, but my head hurts like hell. You okay, Paige?"

She nodded, cupping her drink. When she finally

looked at him, he was surprised to see uncertainty reflected back. "I'll be fine," she said, turning to Angela. "Now that we're all here, why don't you tell us what happened last night?"

"Well, Jake says he remembers an envelope, and leaving the house. I left that for him, and asked him to meet me outside Abernathy's house around midnight. He did, and we watched Trent drug a woman - Alice Burton - and take her into his house. He called you, you came in time to see the woman come back out of the house, and you left. Jake and I took Alice to the hospital, he dropped me off at my car, and I went home." She paused, taking another sip of coffee. "That's what I was involved with. But I have a theory about what happened later."

"So Jake and I were both with you after midnight? Watching Abernathy?" Paige frowned. "Did he know we were there?"

Angela nodded slowly. "He knows I watch him. And he saw us in the car."

Paige set her cup down, her eyes narrow as she stared at the counter. Jake could almost see the gears turning in her mind.

"And I left before you took the other woman to the hospital," she said. Angela nodded again. "I probably went to check out the house then. So that explains how Abernathy got a hold of me. Jake must have gone looking around after he dropped you off."

"That's what I was thinking," Angela confirmed.

She pushed her cup away and looked at Paige. "I thought we could go talk to Alice this morning, the woman we took to the hospital. That's why I came over..."

Jake looked up at the hesitation in her voice. "But?"

"I called the hospital while you two were getting ready. She checked out early this morning with a man who identified himself as her husband."

Paige perked up, her head turning sharply toward Angela. "Did he match Abernathy's description?"

"No." Angela sighed. "The man the nurse described was completely different. Unfortunately for us, Alice Burton isn't married."

Agent Paige pulled her phone out of her pocket. "Maybe we'll just stop by Ms. Burton's house and see if she's home." Hitting a few keys, she held the phone to her ear and looked at Jake. "I need something to write on."

Jake got up and brought back a pad and pen from the living room. He passed them to her as she spoke with someone on the phone. The motions felt wrong somehow, like something was missing. Paige scribbled something on the notepad and hung up, dropping the pen on the counter.

Just like that, it clicked into place. She never used paper. Ever.

"Where's your tablet computer?" he asked, glancing around the counters in case he'd missed it.

Paige frowned, looking at Angela. "Did you see it when you came in?"

Angela shook her head. "No, but I wasn't really paying attention, since you were on the floor. When was the last time--" she stopped, grinning sheepishly. "Right. Maybe if we replay the most likely scenario from last night." She slide off the stool and headed toward the front door, but stopped and turned back, brows drawn together. "Do you have a back door?"

Jake pointed to an open door five feet away. "There's a door to the garage through there, and one off the deck in back. Would he have carried us all the way around back? Assuming we didn't walk, that is."

"No harm in checking both," Paige said, stepping past him and walking into the laundry room. "I don't--oh wait."

Standing just outside the door, he saw her pick up the slim black pad from its perch on the washer. "That was easy enough. You must have put it down when--"

The look on her face silenced him. Angela slipped around him and through the door, hurrying to look over Paige's shoulder. The agent tried to tip the screen away, but she was too late, judging from Angela's horrified gasp.

Paige reached out to hand Jake the screen. "I didn't leave it here," she said as he took it from her shaking hand. "He left it there for me."

Certain he didn't want to see, but unable to resist,

Jake looked down at the video loop that had just started over at the beginning based on the control screen at the bottom. The first part was chilling enough as the camera panned over Paige in his bed as she slept. He wondered briefly where he'd been. The shot cut away for an instant, and a woman's bare feet appeared, secured with duct tape just above the ankles. A buzzing sound in the background grew louder, until the long blade of a reciprocating saw moved into the frame. Dim light glinted off a silver ring on the finger holding the trigger down. The feet twitched, and Jake realized suddenly that whoever owned them was still alive as the blade bit across the ankles and the screaming began. Unable to watch more, he set the device face-down on the counter and leaned against the door frame as he tried to catch his breath.

The awful noise stopped abruptly. Jake looked up to find both women staring at him, an equal mixture of shock and fear on their faces. He rubbed his sweaty palms on his jeans, noting that they both watched his movement. Glancing down, his stomach turned as the realization hit.

Same ring. Same finger.

Chapter Nine

Trent hummed to himself as he worked, hunched over the counter in his lab. It had taken most of the day, but as he slid the supple skin over the bones he'd cleaned and covered with natural fiber padding, he knew it had been worth the extra time. Last time he'd been in too much of a hurry, and the skin had rotted right there on poor Angel's feet. This time he'd gone back to his taxidermy roots, to make sure they wouldn't need another donor for several months.

Not for Angel, in any case.

Clearing off the counter, he washed his hands well, and then wiped down the entire lab, just as he always did. Taking the trash bag, he turned out the lights, leaving Angel's new feet on the counter to cure. They should be ready for her in a couple of days.

After a trip to the incinerator in the shed out back, he washed his hands again and made his way into the

91

cellar room to check on his patient. Or *their* patient, he thought, smiling as he remembered how easily Dr. Werner had been compelled to "help". This latest experiment was proving to be quite intriguing, and it would only take a few more tests before it was ready to market. Those government lab rats would pay a pretty penny for it, he'd bet, just as they had for the last concoction he'd given his contact to sell. Too bad they hadn't bothered to read his instructions carefully before trying to whip up another batch.

He reached the bottom step, pleased to see she was awake. "How are you feeling, my dear?" he asked as she turned to look at him. She frowned, considering the question.

"I'm not sure." She glanced at her feet...or the guaze wrapped stumps where they used to be, then back at him. "Something must have happened to me, but I can't remember what it was. Do you know?" Her eyes glistened with tears as she waited.

He stroked his chin with one hand. "I may be able to help you. But would you mind if I asked you a few questions first?"

"I guess not."

"Excellent." Trent pulled on a pair of latex gloves and sat by her side on a wheeled stool. He took one of her hands in his. "We'll start with something simple. Do you remember your name?"

"Eva Winston." Relief was evident in her voice as she answered without hesitation.

He smiled encouragingly, rubbing his thumb in circles over the back of her hand. "It's nice to meet you, Eva. You can call me Trent. What's the last thing you remember about last night?"

She thought for a moment. "I got off work and went home."

"And what time was that?" He kept stroking her hand, waiting as if he had nothing but time.

She shook her head. "I'm not sure. Six, maybe? It's kind of fuzzy right now."

"That's perfectly all right. You're doing great. Do you remember going to bed?"

A tear slipped down her cheek. "N--no...I guess I don't. What's happening to me? Why can't I remember?"

"There, there now. Let me get you something to help you rest. Then we'll figure it out together." He patted her shoulder and got a pre-filled syringe from the work bench. "This will sting just a bit..."

She winced as he injected the amber liquid, but it wasn't long before her eyelids drooped and her head lolled to the side. He got a stethoscope and held it to her chest, listening to her heartbeat fade. When it stopped, he looked down at her for a moment, so peaceful. Prosthetics had come a long way, and she might have lived a normal life, but considering where he'd found her she wouldn't have been able to afford them anyway.

Letting out a long sigh, he bent down to pull the

plastic sheet up over her body, then went to the other side and did the same. Securing the plastic with tape, he checked his watch. It was still too early to dispose of the body. Perhaps he'd get a bite to eat first.

* * *

Jake sat at an interrogation table for the second time that week, not even trying to keep his foot from tapping nervously on the floor. He knew the only reason he wasn't in lock-up right now was Agent Paige's influence, though she and Angela were both being debriefed as well. Grateful as he was, he couldn't help wondering if he belonged with the other prisoners. Supposedly the lab was checking now to see if his hand matched the one in the video, but the ring was definitely his. He rotated it on his finger, barely refraining from yanking it off and tossing it across the room.

The door opened, and a tall, skinny guy in a dark navy suit walked in. He leaned against the mirrored two-way glass across from Jake and thumbed thoughtfully through a manila folder. Jake wanted to roll his eyes. The agent couldn't possibly be more cliché if he tried.

"Your partner has been very helpful," the agent said, not deigning to look at Jake. "There are just a few more loose ends that we think you'll be able to tie up."

Jake leaned forward, surprised. "Really? Did she remember what happened?"

The man shrugged noncommittally. "Things are starting to come together. With your help--"

Right. Jake suddenly realized the game, finally. Normally he would have caught on from the beginning, but the past few hours had really sent his mind reeling. He looked up to find the agent watching him patiently.

"I'm sorry, could you repeat the question?"

The slight smirk on the man's lips made Jake want to punch him. "There isn't really a question, Dr. Werner. I just need to know exactly what you remember about last night. Your partner told us most of the story, but we need your side to see if it matches up."

Jake sat back in his chair. "I don't remember anything about last night, really. The last thing I remember is leaving my house to meet someone, presumably Angela Redding. The next thing was waking up with the headache from hell this morning. Everything in between is completely blank, like I said in my statement."

The agent sighed, tossing the file on the table and taking a seat. Hands folded on the hard surface, he leaned in as if sharing a secret. "Come on now, Dr. Werner. We both know that's not true. Not according to your partner, anyway. Ms. Redding--"

"Ms. Redding and I are acquaintances, nothing more. I assumed you were referring to Agent Paige, whom I've been working a case with."

The man sat back in his chair, disapproval on his face. "Does it matter? The fact is, you know where you were last night, do you not?"

"I only know what Angela told me. Half of which was speculation. I have no memory of the events that she pieced together based on supposition."

"And the video from this morning? Do you remember cutting a woman's feet off, Dr. Werner?"

Looking him straight in the eye, Jake didn't hesitate. "No."

The agent stood and walked around the table. He peered down, looming. "Have you ever thought about cutting off a woman's feet?"

"No I haven't," Jake said, calmly leaning back in his chair. "Have you?"

A navy jacket pocket trilled, and the man stepped back, pulling his phone out to look at the screen. Sliding it back in his pocket, he gathered up the file and went to the door. Before he left, he looked back over his shoulder. "Stick around, Dr. Werner. Things just got a little more interesting."

* * *

Half an hour later, Agent Paige opened the door. Her hair was loosely pulled back at the base of her neck, her skin was paler than normal, and her eyes

were dull and tired. She didn't come in, just held the
door open.

"Come on," she said quietly. "I'll take you home."

Jake followed her out, past the curious stares of her
co-workers. She was silent all the way to the car, and
finally when she closed her door and slid the key in
the ignition, he couldn't stand it anymore.

"You look like hell," he said, earning a brief flash
of her normal fire in a glance as she pulled out of the
lot. *Better.* "So why did they let me go? What did the
lab results say?"

She stared straight ahead, taking two more turns
before answering. "The video analysts are nearly one
hundred percent sure that while it is your hand holding the saw in the video, the woman's feet were
spliced in later. So it's unlikely that you were the one
to...commit that particular crime."

Relieved as he was, he could sense that there was
something else. Something big they needed to discuss.
"Thank god. What else?" he said, earning a slightly
surprised look. "I know there's something you're not
telling me, Kate. Your body language is screaming
that loud and clear."

Paige pulled into his driveway and cut the engine.
Resting both hands on the wheel, she sat quietly for
several moments before inhaling deep, and letting it
out on a long sigh. Glancing at him with glassy eyes,
she looked forward again, avoiding his gaze.

"They did a rape kit on me. The doctor who performed it said that I definitely had intercourse last night, and that it probably wasn't...forced."

Jake slumped back against the seat, letting her words sink in. "I don't suppose you had sex before..."

"No."

"So it was either him or me then. Assuming Angela's right about what happened."

"Yes."

He started to reach out, instinctively wanting to comfort her, but pulled his hand back. It didn't seem appropriate, somehow. She took another deep breath, expelling it in a rush, then turned to look him in the eye. "They'll be testing the DNA sample you gave them back at the office. I had them put a rush on it, so we should know by tomorrow. There's no evidence of condom use, so..."

"I'm clean," he offered, though the words felt shallow in light of the situation.

"I am too. We'll hope that's the only problem we have to deal with."

He nodded, not wanting to think about the other issues. "So what do we do now? What about the blood tests for drugs? Did they find anything in our systems?"

"Not a trace," she said, frustration in her voice. "Whatever he gave us, it's gone now, and no one has any idea what kind of substance would do that. If that's what happened. He could have hypnotized us instead..."

Jake shook his head, frowning. "I think we can safely rule that out. Hypnotism doesn't really work that way." He ran a hand through his hair. "There only seems to be one real solution to figure all this out, and Abernathy is obviously in the center. We need to get in that house. I don't suppose there's enough for a warrant?"

"No." Her brows drew together in thought. "But if Angela's right, and we got in once, we should be able to do it again." Yawning wide, she shot him a tired look. "We should probably get some sleep first though." Her face flushed, and she looked away. "Separately, I mean."

"Hey." He waited until she looked at him to continue. "I don't remember anything at all, so no offense, but it's like it never happened. Okay?"

"Right," she said brusquely. "I should go. I'll call you tomorrow. About Abernathy, I mean."

He got out of the car and watched her drive away, wondering if there was a man alive who could talk to a woman without offending her.

Jake went in the house long enough to pull on black long-sleeved tee shirt and retrieve Abernathy's address. Tucking a digital camera in his pocket and leaving a note on the kitchen counter, he went to his car, determined to get the information they needed. After last night, he was convinced Abernathy was involved. They needed evidence, and he was going back to the house to get it. He'd wait until Abernathy left, and then take pictures of everything he could. If he was lucky, he'd be out again before Abernathy returned home. If not, he'd hope either Kate or Angela would see the note on his counter.

He parked two blocks away and walked through the alley across the street until he found a good vantage point behind a tall set of lilac bushes. He sat down, huddled in the brush as he watched and waited.

Late afternoon turned to evening. Lights came on in the surrounding houses, and every so often Jake would see a brief flare in Abernathy's mansion. What did the man do in there all day, he wondered? Then the image in the video rose in his mind again, unbidden, and he shivered. Whatever it was, he'd find out soon enough.

Two hours later, Jake watched as a long, wide touring car pulled out of the gates and turned onto the street. He waited five more minutes before he crept up between the two houses he'd been watching between and peered out at the quiet street. Satisfied that the car was gone, he ran across and went around the side of the estate. There were a couple logs stacked against the fence and he used them to swing up and over, landing feet-first behind Abernathy's garage.

A brief sense of deja vu hit him, and he glanced at his surroundings. Was this the way he'd entered the estate before? He shook it off and started moving again. It was probably natural that he'd follow the same path, since something had led him to take that route the first time.

He followed the garage wall to the corner and carefully peered around the corner, quickly pulling back. His pulse pounded as he carefully looked again. A basic black sedan was parked in front of the closed garage door, the trunk standing open. Obviously someone was still here, but as far as Jake knew, Abernathy had no close friends, and few family members on speaking terms. It didn't make sense that he would have left someone at the house, so it must have been a visitor Jake had seen leaving.

Flattening himself against the side of the garage, he took a few deep breaths and considered his options. The smart thing would be to turn around and get the hell out of there before he was discovered. He could go back to his hiding place and wait until the sedan left. As long as Abernathy hadn't already been alerted by a perimeter alarm or something, that would work. He could wait where he was and see what Abernathy was up to, or he could try to sneak past the car and deeper into the estate to hide until Abernathy left.

Brisk footsteps on the concrete drew his attention back to the driveway. Moving now would be foolish, he decided. The risk of being heard was greater than that of being caught. He squatted down and leaned out just enough to see a man the right height and build to be Abernathy approach the trunk. There was a bundle hanging carelessly over his shoulder, and he placed one end in the trunk first, then leaned down to drop the other in as well. Pushing the big door down until the latch clicked loudly, he brushed his hands off on his pants and then retrieved something from his pocket. He opened the driver's door then turned to look in Jake's general direction.

"You may as well come out now, Dr. Werner. I have excellent security on the premises and I was alerted the moment you jumped the fence."

Chapter Ten

Trent grinned at Dr. Werner as the man eased around the corner of the garage. He hadn't expected company again so soon, but given the reality Werner had undoubtedly been dealing with all day, the man probably wanted answers. The video really had been a work of art.

"What can I do for you, Dr. Werner?"

"I was just going to ask you a few questions," Werner said, glancing toward the front of the property. "No one seemed to be answering the call at the gate, so I thought I'd knock on the door instead."

Trent smiled, inclining his head amicably though it was clear from the man's voice he wasn't being entirely truthful. "I see - I'll have the gate checked. Unfortunately, I was just heading out for a few hours, but if you'd care to join me, I'd be happy to talk in the car."

Werner shifted his gaze to the house, down to the trunk of the car and then back to Trent's face. Trent stifled a laugh as he watched conflicting emotions swim in Werner's eyes. It was fun playing with common people, but so much more rewarding to be matched with a fellow intellectual. There was really only one choice, and he suspected Werner knew that.

"That's okay. I'll just stop by later. If you'll excuse me..." Werner started walking toward the driveway.

Bold move. Trent watched him until he was on the other side of the car. Surely Werner didn't think he'd be allowed to stay on or near the estate alone. "Oh come now. Where we speak is irrelevant, is it not? I'd hate for you to have wasted the trip."

Werner considered that for a moment, then nodded. "Of course you're right," he said, pulling the passenger door open. "I appreciate you taking the time."

Trent smiled then slid behind the wheel and waited until Werner's seat belt clicked into place. He pulled slowly out onto the driveway and pushed the button to lock all the doors before exiting the estate. Werner put on a good show of not reacting, but the flinch of his shoulders and his grasp on his own knees were unmistakable. *Good,* Trent thought as he pulled out into traffic. He wanted the therapist to be a little nervous.

At the end of the block, Trent turned onto a main arterial road, and settled into a lane. "So, what did you want to discuss?"

"What is it exactly that you do, Mr. Abernathy?"

Trent gave a half-hearted shrug, considering his answer carefully. "I'm in development," he said, curious to know what had triggered that question. Nearly everyone wanted to know about his money, but it was rare for anyone to ask what he did to earn it. "I create things, research, do testing and then sell it to the highest bidder. My apologies, but I can't say exactly what. Classified, you understand."

"Of course," Werner replied, his expression saying he wasn't buying it for one second. "They must be some big contracts, but then, you don't really need them, do you?"

"No." Trent grinned, finding the indirect approach refreshing. Normally people just came right out and asked how much money he had. "I'm well taken care of by my trust account."

Werner nodded, unfazed. "Mr. Abernathy, have you ever thought about cutting off someone's feet?"

* * *

Jake fought to keep from rubbing his sweaty palms on his pants as he waited for Abernathy's response. It had been a risk, just asking point blank about the feet, but he'd hoped for more of a reaction. Abernathy didn't blink an eye though, just kept driving as though being asked if he'd considered cutting someone's feet off a rather mundane occurrence.

"Not recently," he replied, taking a right turn past the refinery. "Though it sounds like you've given it some thought. There's a name for people with a fetish for feet, Dr. Werner. I can't quite remember the term though."

"Podophilia," Jake said. "That isn't exactly what I was talking about. Although I suppose that someone who cut feet off another person and kept them might fall into that category. I was referring more to the act of dismemberment, and wondering if you'd ever thought about doing that."

Abernathy laughed as he pulled into a gas station just before the last exit to the interstate. "So now you're suggesting I should cut off my own feet? Really, Dr. Werner - you're too amusing for words, but I'm afraid I'll have to cut our chat short. I'm going on a trip, you see, and I'd hate to inconvenience you. But thank you for the fascinating conversation. We'll talk again soon, I presume."

The door locks clicked open, and Abernathy smiled pleasantly, waiting for him to leave. Jake pushed the door open and got out. He wasn't really sure why, but something about Abernathy's relaxed demeanor warned him not to push any further.

"Um, thank y--" Abernathy drove off before Jake could finish the thought, and it was another minute before he realized two things. Abernathy had never actually answered his question, and Jake was miles away from his car.

Cursing under his breath, he fished his cell phone out of his pocket. Just as he found Agent Paige's number, a car pulled up beside him, the passenger window rolled down. He glanced inside and grinned.

"Need a ride?" Paige stared back from the driver's seat, looking annoyed. He pulled the door open and slid in, barely closing it as she hit the gas. Turning onto the exit ramp, she drove in the same direction Abernathy had.

Jake squirmed in his seat. The standard *"Hi, How are you?"* didn't quite seem appropriate at this point. "So I guess you were following Abernathy too?"

She stared out into the darkness, her lips set in a thin line.

Oh.

"You were following me." He ran a hand through his hair, letting out a long breath. "So all that bullshit before, about how it wasn't likely that I actually cut that girl's feet off - that wasn't true?"

"I know you didn't do that."

He shook his head. "Why follow me then?"

She sighed, glancing at him briefly before looking back at the road. "Because I knew you'd go back there. And I wasn't sure...I thought it was possible you were working with him somehow. That would explain the video."

"So why pick me up then?"

"If you were working with Abernathy, he wouldn't have any reason to leave you behind. Based on the shape of the object he put in the trunk, I think he's going to dump the body." Paige tossed a small camera into Jake's lap. "And we're going make our own video."

Jake held the camera as Paige followed Abernathy's taillights down the highway. Traffic was sparse and Paige kept them only close enough to see the red dots in the distance. Uneasy, Jake shifted in the seat. Something was wrong with the whole situation. Even if Jake hadn't followed right away, Abernathy had to know that they'd drive this stretch of road as soon as possible, since Jake had seen the direction he'd taken. Granted, there was a lot of public land this far out of town and plenty of hills and valleys to hide in, but Abernathy had always seemed overly cautious, and Jake didn't see any reason why he wouldn't be now.

Unless he was baiting them.

"I think we should go back," Jake said. "Something doesn't feel right. He's letting us follow him for a reason."

Paige shrugged. "It's possible. Either way, I'd like to see where we end up. Any information we can get would help."

"As long as he doesn't kill us, you mean?"

She didn't answer, just stared down the highway, and he settled back into the seat. The red lights disappeared around a curve, and when they reached the next stretch of highway, he couldn't see them anymore.

"Where'd he go?" Jake asked, peering into the darkness. "Is there another turn ahead?" He tapped the GPS unit attached to the dash and brought it back to life, their current route flashing on the screen. The highway looked straight for the next several miles, and the raw feeling in his stomach grew worse. "That was the last turn for a while. He must have stopped somewhere."

"Keep an eye out," Paige instructed, speeding up a little. "I bet he pulled off the road somewhere in here. Watch the shoulder."

Jake stared out the window, straining into the darkness as he looked for a likely spot to turn off at. He glanced up just in time to see a flash of yellow light illuminating a rear window fifty yards off the road or so.

"There," he said pointing a thumb over his shoulder. "I saw a light - a dome light back there away from the highway. It looked like there might have been a gravel road there. We need to turn around."

Paige shook her head, continuing forward. "If we stop too soon, he'll know we were following. It will work better to get farther away and double back on foot."

"Won't that take too long?" Jake thought about the scrub brush they'd have to go through among other things inherent to wild areas they'd have to watch out for. "What if he's gone by the time we get there?"

"Then we'll video the area, and dig up whatever

he's dropping off. Either way, we still both saw him drive out here, and I'm pretty sure whatever it is he's doing, it's not good." She pulled off on another side road and drove past an old farmhouse that looked abandoned. She parked behind a large barn and they got out.

"Got the camera?" she asked, slipping her digital tablet into a slim case and hanging the strap across her body.

Jake nodded. "Got it. And the GPS too, so we don't get lost."

"Okay. Let's go find Abernathy."

* * *

Twenty minutes later, Jake stopped beside Agent Paige. She'd ducked behind a large sage bush and was pointing ahead and to the right. About twenty yards away he could make out a figure moving around in the distance, though it was too dark to make out any features. Muted noises drifted toward them, scuffling and dragging in the dirt.

"Get the camera," she whispered, never taking her eyes off the target. He pulled the device out of his pocket and pushed the power button, releasing three digital notes into the nearly still night. His pulse jumped at the noise, and Paige dropped to her knees, pulling him down by the wrist. He started to apologize, but she shook her head, holding a finger to her lips.

Up ahead, the noises and movement had stopped. Tension nearly crackled in the air and Jake barely breathed as he watched for any sign at all that Abernathy was coming for them. He glanced around, looking for any available hiding places, but the area was mostly open, with short brown grasses and a few brave trees. Beside him, Paige eased a hand behind her back, her fingers closing around the solid grip of her gun.

The slam of metal against metal cracked through the night, and Jake jumped. A yellow light came on, illuminating the inside of Abernathy's car as he got in and shut the door, plunging himself into darkness again. The engine roared and wheels spun in the soft ground as he drove back to the highway, speeding away from town again.

Jake let out his breath in a whoosh, and Paige slowly pushed off the ground. "Come on," she said, already moving forward. "Let's see what he left us."

When they reached the site, Paige swore under her breath. Jake peered over her shoulder into the freshly dug rectangular hole that Abernathy hadn't even bothered to fill in. It was empty.

Paige held out her hand for the camera. "I'll get a picture of this. Look around and see if there's any evidence that he might have dug other graves in the area."

He handed her the device, shaking his head. "I know most serial killers have favorite dumping spots, but Abernathy would know that. I get the feeling that he doesn't even dispose of each body the same way."

"If he's the killer we're looking for, you mean."

Jake rubbed his neck with his hand. "That hole is perfectly sized for a body. Are you trying to tell me he could have just been burying the trash out here? And if that was the case, why did he run?"

She leaned down, peering into the farthest corner of the opening. "Maybe he did leave the trash." She stepped into the void and held the camera up, taking a picture in a bright flash that illuminated a white plastic bag in one corner. Handing the camera to Jake, she picked up the bag and set it back outside the hole, then crawled up to sit beside it.

Jake held her phone over the bag as she pulled the knot open. As she opened the top, Jake snapped a picture of the contents, the flash casting a garish light over a collection of bones, bits of connective tissue and bright red muscle still attached.

Chapter Eleven

Trent hummed quietly as he took the next exit off the highway. He drove five miles, then turned onto a gravel road, his headlights illuminating only a few feet ahead of the car. The road was badly rutted, and he made a mental note to have it graded within the week. It had been several months since he'd last come out, but perhaps it was time to disappear for awhile. As much fun as it was playing with Agent Paige and Dr. Werner, he was getting tired of their constant presence. And Angel would appreciate the cool country air.

The road curved sharply and he pulled up in front of the cabin, cutting the engine with a sigh. He hadn't planned to spend the night away from Angel, but it seemed he had no choice now. Paige and Werner would be photographing his fake burial site about now, and it would be easier to simply disappear for a few hours.

He pushed a button on the dash and heard the tell-tale click of the trunk opening. He got out and locked his door, dropping his keys in his pocket as he went to the back of the car. Tossing the corpse over his shoulder, he carried it to a small shed a few feet away, laying his burden just inside the door. Making two more trips, he locked the door and closed the trunk, then let himself in the cabin. He'd take care of the burials before morning, but a snack and a cup of tea were in order first.

An hour later, he went out the back door with a shovel. It wasn't far to the small cemetery, and he stood at the fence for a few minutes, looking out over the small white markers set in the ground that glowed in the moonlight. One for every victim, though some remains were only ashes, buried in simple cardboard boxes. Still, a better send-off than any of them would have gotten otherwise. Their lives had been worthless until he'd made use of them. A proper burial was the least he could do for their contributions.

Entering the gate, he looked at the layout again, this time with a more critical eye. There were two spaces left in the back at the center, but those were reserved. Moving to the right, he carefully peeled the sod back near the fence, two narrow rectangles six feet long and two feet wide. Whistling to himself, he removed four feet of dirt in each, stopping only a few times to rest as the early morning hours waned. The darkness was just starting to break as he finished the last one, and he hurried back down the hill for a cart and the bodies.

As the sun rose large on the horizon he unwrapped each corpse and rolled it into a grave, pausing a moment after before he picked up the shovel again. Refilling the holes always went faster, and he worked quickly, mounding the dirt up and then stomping it down to level. When he couldn't pack anymore in, he replaced the sod and spread the remaining earth in a light layer that would eventually sink back into the ground.

Opening the box he'd brought along with the bodies, he took out two more smooth white headstones, each with "Abernathy" and two recent dates cut into the surface. He placed one on each grave and pressed it down with his foot, then grinned.

"Rest in peace," he said as he closed the gate and pushed the cart back down to the shed.

* * *

"He knew we were following him."

Jake nodded at Agent Paige's observation as they drove back toward the city. Paige had poked through the remains Abernathy had left in the plastic bag long enough to determine by the size that they probably weren't human. They'd hiked back to the car and put the remains in back before deciding to drive back to the city, instead of going after Abernathy. He'd be long gone by now.

"Any chance of us getting a warrant to search his house?" Jake knew it was a long shot, but had to ask anyway.

Paige shook her head. "It's not a crime to bury a small animal - or kill one, for that matter. Which means we've got nothing." She took the exit into the city, taking the main street towards Jake's subdivision. "We've already jeopardized any future case with all the sneaking around. At this point, our best bet is just to keep a close eye on Abernathy and hope he screws up."

Jake watched the streetlights go by as they drove through town in silence. Abernathy didn't just screw up, and there was no reason he would now. If anything, he'd lay low for awhile, or at least until he needed something again. They'd have to bait him, somehow. Before he disappeared, with any luck.

"We need to set a trap. He's not going to mess up on his own - we need to push him into a mistake."

Paige shook her head. "He'll mess up. They all do, eventually. It's just a matter of waiting them out." She pulled into his driveway, and killed the engine. "Here you go," she said, glancing his way, then quickly looking back at the garage. "I'll come by tomorrow and we can go get your car."

"Thanks." He took his keys out of his pocket and fingered them as the tension grew in the small space.

"You'll...ah, let me know how that test comes out, right?"

She hesitated, then gave him a slight nod. "Of course."

He got out then, and watched her drive away before letting himself in the front door and locking the deadbolt behind him. Toeing off his shoes, he shuffled into the kitchen. The clock on the microwave read two in the morning, and he knew he should get some sleep, but went to the fridge for a beer anyway. Twisting off the top he guzzled half before going to the living room and settling on the couch.

Kate was wrong. Abernathy wasn't going to mess up. Jake turned on the TV but left it muted, sitting back to stare at the images as his mind worked to figure out how they could bait Abernathy. He thought about the two crimes they were reasonably sure Abernathy had committed - taking Megan's eyes, and cutting off a pair of feet. It occurred to Jake that with both crimes, a body part had been removed, and at least in Megan's case, hadn't been found anywhere. Why would Abernathy need random body parts? What was he doing with them?

Shaking his head, Jake set the bottle down, leaned back and closed his eyes to think. Abernathy wasn't an idiot - far from it. There was a reason for his actions. They just had to figure out what it was.

* * *

Loud, insistent pounding woke Jake several hours later. Bright sunlight streamed in through the windows as he blinked, pushing off the couch to stumble to the door and wrench it open.

"Oh good, you're up," Angela said, pushing past him and walking to the kitchen. "You're not going to believe this. Any of it, but I have pictures. We need to call Agent Paige." She tossed a manila envelope on the counter in front of him, and crossed her arms over her chest. "It's...well, just look. Or maybe you shouldn't." She started moved away from the counter, pacing nervously across the room as Jake tried to shake off the last of the fuzziness. Opening the envelope, he pulled out a stack of photos printed on plain printer paper and spread them out on the counter. Bracing his hands on either side, he stared at them, willing the images to make sense. Angela kept pacing on the other side of the counter, the constant movement distracting him.

"Have a seat," he said, bending further down to examine the pictures. "Tell me what I'm looking at here." She snatched one of the pages and held it up for him, pointing to a spot near the right side. It looked like a jar sitting on a shelf.

"Don't you see it? Those are eyeballs, Jake. Real eyeballs!" She handed over the paper and continued pacing. "That whole shelf holds body parts - eyes and feet and hands and organs..." She stopped long enough to point a finger an image of a room. "This is where he works. It's in the basement. There's a metal table, and a drain in the center of the room, and tools..." Her voice trailed off on the last word, and finally Jake's brain decided to engage.

"You went to Abernathy's house? Inside?"

She flung her hands up. "That's what I've been trying to tell you!" Grabbing the back of a chair, she hung on for dear life, her eyes looking past Jake at some unknown target. "I was outside last night, watching like I always do. I saw you sneak in, and then you both drove away. I knew he was gone, and you were with him, so I went over and broke a basement window to get in. We needed evidence and I got it."

Jake noted her white knuckles and pale face. Her agitation made sense now. He went around the counter and pulled her into his arms, rocking her side to side as she clung to him, trembling. He rubbed her back in slow circles, knowing it would take a while for the adrenaline to wear off. He couldn't believe she'd put herself in that position, especially having been kidnapped before.

"Am I interrupting?"

Jake looked up to find Agent Paige standing a few feet away, her expression cold. He shook his head as Angela eased out of his embrace. "Not at all. Angela had a rough night. But --"

Paige held up one hand, palm out. "No need to explain. I just came by to tell you the results are back." She looked into his eyes and laid a piece of paper on top of the photos. "It was you, not that it matters." She turned to go, and he followed, leaving Angela in the kitchen.

"Kate, wait." He reached over her to shut the door she'd nearly pulled open. "It's not like that. And obviously it does matter, but we'll have to deal with that later. You need to see what Angela brought over this morning. It's about Abernathy."

She turned, frowning as she tried to brush past him. "What is it? Does she have evidence?"

"We *will* talk about this later," he said, refusing to move his arm until she finally nodded. He finally moved aside, and she practically jogged back to the kitchen. He shook his head and took a deep breath. *Women.* When he got back to the kitchen, Angela and Paige were both leaning over the counter, studying the photos.

"You shouldn't have gone in there alone," Paige was telling Angela as they looked over the photos. Jake sat on a stool on the other side of the counter, examining an image from a room that looked like a library. He held it close to his face, struggling to make out the figure behind the glare of glass between shelves.

"What is that?" he asked, turning the photo around and pointing.

Angela took it from him, and then reached for another page from the collection, handing it to him. "This is the most disturbing thing I saw. I don't think she's alive, or I hope not, but she breathes..."

Jake frowned as he studied the woman in the glass case. "I guess that would explain why he takes specific parts from his victims." Dropping the photo, he looked at Agent Paige. "Is this enough to get a search warrant? Or at least enough for the FBI to take the case seriously?"

She shook her head. "Unless we can prove he killed people outside the city, it's the jurisdiction of the local police. And since Angela broke into his house to get the photos, none of them can be used as evidence. About all we can do is contact the locals and give them what we have so far."

Angela looked up. "We can't just let him keep doing this. Who knows when he'll go after someone else?"

"Unfortunately, I think I do," Jake said, bracing both hands against the countertop. "Last night he said he had excellent security on the premises. I think we have to assume that he knows you were in the house, and maybe even that you took these pictures."

"Which means I'm next," she said, sinking onto an empty stool. "I felt him. Watching, while I was in the house. What if he was there?"

"You wouldn't have made it out," Paige said, gathering the print-outs into a pile. "But you did, and now we know exactly what we're up against, which is more than we knew before. These are digital, right?" Angela nodded, looking a little stunned as she took the card Paige held out. "Will you email them to me at this address? I'll contact the local authorities, but I'm going to have our people look over these photos too. Maybe we can find something to link him to one of our cases."

"Okay," Angela replied. "But what about me? If Abernathy knows I've been in his house..."

"Is there somewhere you could go? Someone out of town you could visit?" Paige asked.

Angela shook her head. "Not really. Besides, I don't want to run away. Not again."

"Maybe we can use this," Jake said. "We know he's got Angela in his sights, so let's set up a trap for him. If we catch him trying to abduct her, that would at least be grounds to arrest him, right?"

Paige nodded. "It would get us a search warrant too. The problem is, we have no idea when he'll go after her. And more importantly, we can't ensure your safety, Angela."

"Most of his victims are homeless," Jake said. "Except Alice Horton, who he lured back to his house, and Megan, who he targeted at home. If I had to guess, I'd say he'll try to lure Angela into his house. He knows she watches him just about every night. He'll use that to his advantage."

"Stay here for now," Paige told Angela. "And stay

away from Abernathy's place. I'll see what we can set up and call you, but it's important that you stay put. Understand?"

Chapter Twelve

Trent pushed the play button on the remote, staring thoughtfully at the screen hanging in the living room of his cabin. Clearly he should have gone back to town last night instead of waiting for daylight. It's possible Angela could have been spared if she hadn't been so damn thorough, but she'd found and photographed Angel. There was no choice now but to move Angel here to the cabin with him, and integrate her namesake as he'd planned to do all along. It was time.

He turned off the TV and went into the small room near the back door where shelves of electronic equipment sat blinking. Running his finger down the labels, he found the correct receiver and turned it on, adjusting the volume as Dr. Werner's voice came through the speaker. He'd planted the bug the night he returned Werner and the FBI agent to his house and he'd tuned in just in time. The corners of his lips lifted in a half-grin as he listened. When all had grown silent, he turned the receiver off and went to get his jacket. Apparently they still wanted to play, and he was more than willing to take up the challenge.

An hour later he pulled up behind his mansion and let himself in the back gate. He walked briskly to the back door and let himself in, knowing there was little time to waste. Everything had to be taken care of before nightfall. He went downstairs to the surgical suite first and touched a panel in a narrow space between the shelves. The little used gears groaned and squeaked as two tall rectangular portions of the wall swung in, revealing a narrow concrete space tall and long enough for the shelving units to fit in side by side. Going to the far corner of one unit, he swung it out into the middle of the room on squeaky hinges until it was perpendicular to the first door, then pushed it into the space. Repeating the process with the second shelf, he gathered up all of his tools and stowed them on a lower shelf in the tiny bunker. Stepping outside, he touched the panel again and the doors swung shut, fitting so perfectly together that even the seams were invisible.

Turning off the lights and locking the door, he jogged up the stairs to his bedroom and entered the panic room, relieved that his nosey guest hadn't snooped quite far enough. Making a few adjustments to the security settings, he locked that room down, and then replaced the wall panel and spread the clothing so it would hang in front, just in case. He packed a bag and went out into the hall again, this time headed for his beloved lab. Pity that whoever finally came in to fingerprint it wouldn't respect the near-sterile conditions he tried to maintain there.

Leaving his bag just outside the door, he went straight to the back wall and turned on the hydraulics to lower Angel from her glass room. When she was finally on her back, he leaned over her and gently brushed her hair away from her face.

"We're going to the country for the winter, Angel. I think you'll be pleased with the view I've set up for you. The ride may be a little bumpy, so I apologize for any discomfort."

He wheeled a gurney frame to her side, and unfastened the hardware that secured her board to the wall. Reaching across he pulled her onto the metal transport and secured the board she lay on with straps. Draping a sheet over her body, he pushed the button that would return the wall to it's upright position then pushed Angel ahead of him into the hall. Grabbing his bag on the way, he entered a wide lift at the back of the house that took them down to ground level. The doors on the opposite side opened into a shed at the back of the property, and he pushed Angel's gurney into the back of a waiting hearse.

* * *

Jake finished putting the dishes in the dishwasher, and turned it on. Brushing the light switch off on his way out, he went to the living room where Angela had fallen asleep shortly after dinner. They'd spent the day trying to come up with a suitable way to draw Abernathy out with the least amount of risk to her, but in the end, the plan that seemed most likely to work was also the most dangerous. Angela would go and watch the house like she always did, while a support team from the local police office would wait a few blocks away to avoid detection. They couldn't predict whether Abernathy would try to talk her into the house, or if he would just drug her, but either way, Jake and Paige would be videotaping the whole thing from the hiding spot he'd used the other night. When Paige gave the signal, police would arrest Abernathy, and they'd call for the promised search warrant.

Unfortunately, the local office didn't have the people to spare until the next night, so they had to hold off one more day. Paige had left a few hours ago to get some sleep, and suggested they both do the same.

Spreading a quilt over Angela, Jake noticed how drawn and pale her face was, even in sleep. He didn't blame her. The thought of facing Abernathy again was chilling, to say the least. He went around the house checking doors and windows to make sure

127

everything was locked, even though he'd done the same thing right after Paige left. Satisfied that it was as secure as he could make it, he pulled the comforter off his bed and stretched out in a large chair across from Angela in the living room. Abernathy was smart, and he'd gotten into the house before.

A quiet knock sounded from the front door, and he tossed the blanket off and went down the hall, careful not to turn on any lights or make any noise. Looking through the peephole, he allowed himself to breathe again and opened the door for Agent Paige.

"I couldn't sleep," she said, stepping inside. "I kept thinking Abernathy would make a play here, so I decided to just come over."

Jake locked the door and nodded. "I had the same thought. Angela's asleep, but I think it's because she finally just passed out from exhaustion." He followed her into the living room, where she looked at the other woman for a minute, then continued down the hall and into the kitchen. She reached for the light switch, then pulled her hand back without turning it on.

"Do you mind if we keep it dark?" She slid onto a stool, her shadow backlit by the small amount of light put out by a nightlight in the laundry room.

"Not at all," he said, taking a seat next to her. "Want coffee or anything?"

She leaned forward, bracing her forearms on the counter top. "I want to apologize...for earlier," she said, her voice so low he had to lean in to hear. "I don't normally...I shouldn't have gotten upset when I came in earlier today. It's none of my business, and it really doesn't even matter. I'm not...I don't get emotionally involved. This whole case is just..."

"I know." He refrained from touching her hand, though just barely. "For what it's worth, at least it wasn't that scumbag. And there really is nothing going on between me and Angela."

"It doesn't matter. I just didn't want you to think I--"

He chuckled. "What, that you care? That the great FBI Agent Kate Paige isn't attracted to me? I think we both know that's not true."

"It wouldn't be professional to get involved - you know that as well as I do, Dr. Werner. Or you should, given your occupation."

He nodded, intrigued by this display of uncertainty from her. "Except you're not my client, and I'm just a consultant with your office. Does the FBI have rules against fraternization with consultants?"

She shook her head. "I don't know, and that's not the point. I just think we need to keep things...professional."

Jake decided to take pity on her. For now. "Well I'm not paying you, if that's what you're after," he said lightly, not even flinching when she smacked him in the arm. Dark as it was, he could make out a slight smile on her face. Good.

His cell phone rang, and he answered quickly so

the noise wouldn't wake Angela. The line was silent for several seconds, and he held a finger to his lips as he frowned at Paige.

"Good evening, Dr. Werner." Abernathy's voice crawled over Jake's skin like sandpaper, and he pressed the speakerphone button so Paige could hear. "I have a proposition for you."

Jake hesitated until Paige gestured he should keep talking, the phone giving off enough light to illumin-ate her actions.

"I'm listening," he said, frowning. He hadn't expec-ted Abernathy to make the first move, and judging from he look on Kate's face, she hadn't either.

Abernathy cleared his throat. "Very good. I'd like to invite you and your lady-friends over to the house for dinner tomorrow night. It seems we may have gotten off on the wrong foot, and I'm sure it's my fault. Since you all seem to have taken an interest in the property, perhaps a tour afterwards, as a sign of goodwill?"

Jake looked at Paige, who nodded after a few seconds of thought. "That's...very kind of you," Jake said as Angela shuffled into the room and turned on the light, momentarily blinding him. He held a hand up to signal her to stay quiet. "What time should we be there?"

"Excellent! I think seven is fashionable these days, is it not? I look forward to seeing you, Dr. Werner. Until tomorrow, ladies." The line went dead, and

Jake's vision started to clear as his eyes adjusted to the bright light.

"What did I miss?" Angela took a mug off the counter and held it under the water spigot in the refrigerator door. "I heard Abernathy talking..."

Paige rubbed her hands over her face and sighed. "He invited us to dinner tomorrow night. I don't know what his game is, but it's a way inside, and he's offered us a tour which means he's probably cleaned the place up. All we can hope for is that he missed something."

Angela sipped her water. "So I don't have to go in alone, but what about you guys? And how do we get a search warrant?"

Paige shrugged. "We can't, unless he does or says something that incriminates him." She reached for her digital tablet, her fingers flying over the surface. "I'm going to order wires - we'll all wear one. That way if we get separated for any reason, we still have a way to know what's going on. We already have the team lined up, so I'll have them monitor from down the block, and be ready to rush in if they need to."

"So what do we do until then?" Angela asked, her brows drawn together. "Could this be a ruse to make us relax so he can do something between now and tomorrow night? He called awfully late."

Jake folded his arms over his chest and paced in front of the sink. "I don't think so," he said, mentally reviewing his files on Abernathy. "He likes to play with people, manipulate them. He's probably got the whole evening planned tomorrow, including how to get you..." he looked up at Angela,"...alone."

Her eyes sparkled with unshed tears, and he regretted his words, but it was the truth. Angela was special to Abernathy for some reason, and had been all those years ago. Unfortunately, that meant her betrayal would be taken more seriously too.

"We should all get some sleep," Paige said, tucking the tablet under her arm and retrieving her keys from the counter. "I'll get all the arrangements switched, and meet you back here tomorrow afternoon."

* * *

Jake waited outside the black FBI van as Agent Paige and Angela finished being outfitted with wires. Resisting the urge to scratch his chest where they'd taped the slender cable, he glanced at the neighborhood houses. The black conversion van with no windows was just too obvious - anyone looking out their windows would immediately think there were either kidnappers, terrorists, or FBI agents afoot. Too bad there wasn't a better option for all the equipment needed for surveillance.

The women joined him on the sidewalk and the van's door slid shut with a rather final sound.

"Everyone ready?" Paige asked, and he nodded, noting the drawn lines and dark circles under Angela's

eyes as they started walking toward Abernathy's estate. After Paige had left, they'd both tried to sleep,
and when he gave up and went to the kitchen for a
snack, Angela had been awake as well. They'd spent
the rest of the night watching old black and white
movies on cable. Sometime after dawn they'd both
fallen asleep on the couch, and he'd slept fitfully until
just before noon. Angela had already gotten up by the
time he was stirring.

The imposing mansion loomed large as they approached, the gates to the main drive standing open
two feet. The night was eerily still, not even a breeze
daring to blow as they made their way up to the front
door. It opened almost immediately, and Abernathy
stood just inside, impeccably dressed for dinner in an
expensive black suit and tie.

"Come in!" he said with a generous sweep of the
arm, smiling amicably as they filed past and then closing the door behind. "So glad you could make it. I'm
sure this will be a night to remember for all of us."

Jake dipped his head in acknowledgement and
offered his hand, determined to play along for now.
"Thank you for having us, Mr. Abernathy. It's a pleasure to be here." He watched just the barest hint of
surprise, maybe even a little respect cross the other
man's face. *One point to the psychologist.* Jake didn't have
to fake a smile.

"It's good to be here," Paige said, the words sound-
ing a little forced. Jake watched Abernathy closely as

he bent over her proffered hand and touched it with his lips. Her muscles tensed, but to her credit, she didn't pull away.

"So good to see you again, Madam. Or do you prefer Agent?"

"Agent Paige is fine," she said, retrieving her hand.

Abernathy turned to Angela, bowing formally. "And good evening to you, Ms. Redding. I'm so glad you're here." When she didn't reply, he merely smiled and stepped back. "Shall we adjourn to the dining room? Dinner is ready. This way, please."

Jake followed him into a large, rectangular room with bright yellow walls and an elegant table for twelve. Four places had been set at one end, and Abernathy took the chair at the head, waiting for the ladies to be seated before he pulled his own chair out. Then he rang a small crystal bell, and two servants came through a door in the middle of one long wall, bearing trays with small white bowls on them. One bowl was delivered to each plate, with a dark, pleasantly strong beef aroma that made Jake's mouth water. They'd eaten before arriving, of course, but he still considered taking just a small taste.

"The soup is mushroom, an old family recipe. The morels are especially tasty." Abernathy brought a spoonful to his lips, closing his eyes as he swallowed. "Mmm...perfect. You really should try it." He looked expectantly at them, and Jake leaned forward, ready to address the issue as they'd agreed. But before he could speak, Abernathy rang the little bell again, and the servants returned.

"I believe my guests are reluctant to sample food from my kitchen. It's my fault, of course. Please take a taste of their soups, so they know I haven't altered it to be...well, dangerous to ingest." He waited patiently, his expression serene.

One point to the serial killer, Jake thought as one of the servants produced a spoon and took a small taste from his bowl. After all the soups had been tasted, they went back to the kitchen and Abernathy grinned.

"There now. Please, enjoy the soup."

Agent Paige caught Jake's eye and gave her head a small shake, but he just shrugged and picked up his spoon, taking a small mouthful. Abernathy was testing them, probing for ... something, and maybe if he felt like he was in control ...

Two thumps came from just beyond the kitchen door, and Angela twitched at the sound. "What was that?"

Abernathy laid his napkin beside his plate and leaned back in his chair with a sigh. "Pity they didn't make it just a few seconds longer. Dr. Werner, I'm afraid you just don't really fit in with the rest of my plans for the evening."

Chapter Thirteen

Glancing at the clock on the wall, Trent made a mental note that the timing of the new sedative was off. He'd have to work on the dosage amounts before he handed the formula over next month. Pity. He'd thought that particular project was finished. Fortunately, the error was favorable to tonight's schedule, but he had hoped to keep his guests in the dark a little while longer.

Agent Paige tensed, inching her seat back ever so slowly. Dr. Werner and Ms. Redding were both leaning forward, looking ready to bolt. He'd have to be quick.

"Now, now," Trent said, holding his hands up with what he hoped was an appropriately sheepish grin. "No need to get all excited. We still have much to discuss, and I suspect you may be interested in what I have to show you. So please, sit down and relax. Since

I doubt you have interest in eating - though I can assure you the food is quite safe - allow me to tell you a story."

Agent Paige stood. "I don't think so, Abernathy. Unless you're going to tell us why you murdered those women. And almost murdered Megan Hunter. Why did you let her live, by the way? And I have a whole list of questions just like that, if you're in the sharing mood?"

Trent clapped his hands, the sound echoing through the large room. "Bravo, Agent Paige. Well done." He looked over at his old psychologist, who seemed to be getting a bit sleepy, lolling in his chair. "This one's a firecracker, Werner, don't you agree? You can see why I paired you with her, I hope."

The other man nodded, barely able to keep his eyes open. Angela got up and went over to him, concern in her eyes as she leaned down to look in his face. "What's wrong with him? What did you do?"

Trent shrugged. "Just a little experiment, is all. He'll be fine in around..." he checked his watch, "...three hours from now, I'd think? Though my calculations have been off a little lately..."

"Why just him? Why aren't Angela and I affected?" Paige loomed over him, hands on her hips, and breasts heaving. Perfectly shaped mounds, Trent noted. Maybe when this was over, he'd have use for those. As long as he could get the frame shape correct.

137

"You weren't part of the experiment, my dear. I'm afraid someone has to stay behind - otherwise no one will know where to come looking for you, and that really would be tragic."

"I don't think you have to worry about that, Abernathy. Unless you've already drugged us too, we're not going anywhere. In fact there's a team outside waiting..."

Trent shook his head with a chuckle. "You really don't get it, do you Agent Paige? Of course you have a team outside, and I'm sure you're wearing a wire too - maybe more than one of you. It's all so," he yawned loudly, patting his lips dramatically with one hand, "predictable. But I sincerely doubt I'll require chemical assistance to insure your cooperation this time. I believe your natural curiosity will be incentive enough."

* * *

Jake woke slowly, his eyes fighting to bring the room into focus. Groaning at the pounding between his temples, he sat up in the hard chair at the dining room table, stretching his neck and back with an annoying amount of pain. He was alone, it appeared, and as his brain started working again, he pushed up out of the chair, grabbing the edge of the table as he swayed on his feet.

"Son of a bitch," he muttered, shaking his head as

138

he waited impatiently for the dizziness to pass.
"Abernathy?" he called out, cringing at the volume
but needing to try, though he didn't expect an answer.
Forcing his feet to move, he checked the kitchen, noting the servants must have woke up and gone. Then
he went to the living room. "Kate? Angela?"

Damm it.

He went back to the dining room and surveyed the
table, then ran up the main stairs when he remembered the library and the image from Angela's
pictures. Jogging into the library, he shoved the curtain aside to find the case empty, save for a note
tacked to the inside of the glass written in a flowing
calligraphy script.

*"I trust you had a restful nap, Dr. Werner. I've decided to
finally unveil my art to the world, and I do hope that you will
attend, along with your FBI colleagues as well as any news media outlets who care to send a representative. Perhaps you'll
want to invite that nice Megan Hunter as well. She may have a
particular interest in one of the displays.*

*The unveiling will take place tomorrow evening at eight
o'clock sharp. If you make it on time, I'm sure Agent Paige
will be happy to escort you home. If not...well...I'm afraid she'll
have other plans - indefinitely.*

*The catch, of course, is that you'll need to find your own way
to the party. I've left some clues lying about that should help
you - the first is on the table behind where you are now standing. Good luck, and Godspeed, Dr. Werner. I do hope to see*

139

you there."

Jake turned and picked up the small white envelope from the coffee table, ripping it open to pull out an expensive-feeling card. There was a single sentence typed in the center:

"Take out the trash."

Turning the card over to make sure he didn't miss anything, Jake shoved it in his back pocket and looked around for a garbage receptacle. There was a small one by a large leather cigar chair, but it was empty. He considered checking all of the upstairs bins, but decided that would be a last resort. He'd check the kitchen first, as that was where most people kept a garbage can.

The hunch paid off, and he ripped another white envelope off the front of the bin to find another simple sentence on the card inside:

"Go West thirty-five."

Turning right, then left, Jake decided West was the hall leading past the dining room and toward the back door. Starting beside the garbage, he took normal steps, counting each as he moved out into the hall. He reached the back door at twenty, opened it, and kept going out into the back yard. Thirty-five put him right in the middle of the lawn, no envelope in sight. *Fuck.*

Taking out his phone, he checked the GPS to make sure he'd gotten the direction right. So thirty-five what? He hurried back inside to the kitchen, and looked around the room for any item or piece of artwork that was duplicated, but everything seemed original.

"Think, dammit," he mumbled, closing his eyes for a moment. The house was dead silent, not even the hum of a refrigerator to provide white noise. All he heard was the sound of a clock ticking rhythmically on the wall. *Tick-tock. Tick-tock. Tick-tock...*

Jake opened his eyes.

Time.

"Go West Thirty-Five," he mumbled, fishing in the pocket of his pants for the car keys as he headed for the front door. His hand on the knob, he stopped abruptly. "Minutes or seconds?"

Letting his hand slide away from the smooth metal, he made his way back to the kitchen and stood by the garbage can. Checking the GPS on his phone one more time, he faced west and opened up the stopwatch app. Then he touched the screen to start the clock and started walking at a normal pace. When the clock hit thirty-five seconds, he stopped.

There was a stairwell in front of him, with a card taped just inside on the wall pointing down. Flipping on the light switch, he descended into the basement.

"Déjà vu," he said quietly, following the narrow hall to the last door on the left. His hand shook a little as he pushed the door open and felt for a switch on the wall, illuminating a vast, nearly empty room.

As he stepped tentatively over the threshold, images - impressions, really - flashed through his head. Tall metal shelves against the long bare wall. A metal table over the drain in the center of the floor. The crinkle of plastic sheeting underfoot...and that coppery, nauseating smell.

Then all at once, the memories came crashing down, and Jake pressed his hands on either side of his head as the reality of what had happened that night flooded his mind. There had been a woman strapped to the table, and he and Kate had watched as Abernathy cut off her feet with the saw. Then they'd cleaned up the mess while he cauterized the wounds and bandaged her up. There had been some purpose for the feet, but Jake couldn't remember what it was. Or maybe Abernathy hadn't specified.

Jake shook his head, trying to clear the gruesome images from his head. It felt like a dam had burst, and the deluge of information just kept coming but he didn't really want to remember the rest of the evening. Not just yet, anyways. He had to find Kate and Angela.

Forcing himself to focus, he looked around the room again, this time with purpose. There. A metal table was situated against the back wall, and on top there were several items, including one of the now-familiar white cards. Taking it out of the envelope, he read the next clue.

"South East two hours, then East one hour. Kate

and I will be waiting in the cemetery."

Jake took in a deep breath, then let it out, reminding himself that Abernathy liked to play with people. Manipulation was his specialty, and he was just making sure Jake had enough motivation to come after him quickly. But a cemetery was rather dramatic, and the fact that Angela wasn't mentioned...

Shoving the card in his pocket, Jake ran back down the hall, up the stairs and out the front door. He looked down the block and noted the van was gone. Abernathy had probably made Kate call off the detail. Cutting between houses to the next block over, he got in his car, fired up the engine and drove south east toward the nearest highway exit.

* * *

Jake checked the clock on the dash of the car for what had to be the millionth time. Two-thirty in the morning, and the highway was deserted, aside from his own car. He yawned, thinking he should probably pull over. A heavy metal band was blaring through the speakers, and he had the window down part way to let the cool night air in. Still, he could barely keep his eyes open, and he knew it wasn't safe to be behind the wheel.

But Angela and Kate were out there somewhere with that monster. Jake had to get to them as quickly as possible. Abernathy had given a deadline of eight tonight, which didn't give him much time. It couldn't be too much further though. According to the last clue, he had to drive two hours South East, and one East, and it had been nearly an hour since he turned off. He glanced down at the dash one more time.

When he looked up, the oncoming headlights were too close to avoid.

The crunch of metal and the sensation of weight-lessness were all Jake felt on impact, and when he woke hours later in a strange room, he struggled to remember what had happened.

"Feeling any better, Dr. Werner? That was a nasty accident you were in. Tsk, tsk. I really did think I gave you enough time not to rush."

The voice from the doorway was like cold water to Jake's face and he tried to push himself upright as Abernathy entered the room. His left arm wouldn't work properly, and the pain that shot up through his shoulder when he tried to put any weight on it at all nearly made him pass out. Wincing, he laid back down, afraid to close his eyes lest Abernathy carve him up for parts.

"Where are we?" he asked, his mouth dry and chalky. "How did I get here?"

Setting the tray down, Abernathy held one of the glasses to his lips. "It's just water," he said, not push-ing, but allowing Jake to make the choice. Jake took a small, tentative sip through the straw, then a more confident one. If the other man had wanted to kill

144

him, he'd had ample time to do so by now.

"I heard the crash from my bedroom," Abernathy said, putting the empty glass back on the tray. "I went out to see what had happened, and found you thrown clear. So I brought you here, even though you are deplorably early for the party. I don't suppose you had time to call the press before you left?"

Jake shook his head with a short, nervous laugh. "You really think I'd take the time to call people when people's lives are on the line? Where are they, anyway? What did you do to Angela and Kate?" He sat up again, adrenaline helping him overcome the pain this time. Abernathy stood at the edge of the bed, hands in the pockets of his pressed khakis. At Jake's question, he brought his hands up and rubbed them together, smiling.

"Kate is in the cemetery, waiting for us as I said she would be. I'm afraid Angela is indisposed at the moment, but you'll see her later tonight. The party is in her honor, you know. A birthday party, of sorts."

Chapter Fourteen

The confusion on Dr. Werner's face was gradually replaced by horrific understanding, and Trent inclined his head in a humble nod.

"I see you understand why this is such a moment-ous occasion, though I doubt you really grasp the full significance. I've been working toward this nearly my whole life, and Ms. Redding has been a key player for the larger part. Now, of course, she has the starring role, and I can't say I've ever been more proud." He looked at the clock on the wall and shook his head. "I'm afraid there is much to be done yet though, since you failed to follow my instructions. Just lay back and rest for now. I'll be sure to come get you when we're ready to begin."

He left Dr. Werner on the bed, struggling to get up as Trent closed and locked the door behind him. He laid the key on top of the door jamb, then went to the kitchen and poured a cup of coffee before entering the media room at the back of his cabin. Checking the video feeds, he was pleased to see the FBI forensics team going through his house, looking rather frustrated, he thought. Chuckling, he sat at a small desk near the back of the room and spent the next several minutes finishing the press release he'd started earlier. Finally satisfied, he sent out a fax to all of the local news outlets that invited them to the event of the year. *Hell, probably ten years*, he thought as he sipped his coffee. A small chime sounded from his pocket and he took his cup to the kitchen, carefully rinsing, drying and putting it away before he headed up the back stairs.

Opening the door to a guest room, he quietly slipped inside. The shape on the bed had hardly moved since he'd finished, but he was optimistic that the drugs would wear off soon, and she would soon awake to see what a fabulous upgrade he'd given her.

As he got closer, her legs shifted slightly under the blankets. A good sign.

"Wake up, beautiful," he said, rounding the bed so she wouldn't have to turn over just yet. "It's time to start getting ready for your party. I know you're still a little sore, but I've got something to help with that. You'll feel good as new in no time, I promise."

A low whimper came from under the mop of dark curly hair laying across her face. He'd planned a hydrogen peroxide bleach, but had decided at the last minute that he liked the chestnut coloring that framed her pixie face. Now he reached out to move the silky strands aside, revealing that lovely visage he'd worked so hard to perfect. Even working under such a tight deadline, it was good work, if he did say so himself.

"Come on, open your eyes for me, Angel. I need to check the dye."

She whimpered again, her eyelids fluttering up just a little, then closed, then opening just a crack once more. "It hurts," she whispered, her voice raspy and raw.

Trent clicked a pen light on and examined one eye, then the other. A thin crust lined each lid - a side effect he'd expected, but hoped to avoid. "I see the problem. Let me just irrigate those for you..."

He took a small syringe and filled it with water, gently washing away the dried tears. "There. Try again."

Her long lashes rose to reveal his greatest achievement so far.

"Perfect."

* * *

As the lock snapped into place, Jake finally pushed himself up to a sitting position. Breathing hard, he looked around the room, this time paying close attention to the details and examining the window frame in particular. Forcing the horrific possibilities of what

Abernathy might have already done to Kate and Angela aside, he got to his feet and shuffled across the wood floor to peer through the clear glass.

A steep hill stood about twenty yards straight across from the house, with a small trail that led diagonally up the slope through a copse of trees. An old wooden picnic table sat off to one side, dark stains embedded in the splintered top. To the other side, an old tree of some sort stood sentry, imposingly wide and tall. Shadows stretched long over the manicured grass, and twilight seemed to be approaching fast.

There wasn't much time left. He hesitated for another minute, trying to decide which of the women to go after first. If Kate was in the cemetery, she very well could be dead. Or Abernathy could be holding her until Jake showed up. From the way Abernathy had spoken about Angela, she was probably still alive, though the definition could be debatable, considering the living doll they'd seen back at the mansion. His history with Angela was important though, and Jake decided that of the two, Abernathy would be more likely to keep Angela alive, at least until the party tonight. The decision made, Jake reached for the lock on the window, surprised when it turned easily. A few deep breaths, and he climbed out over the sill, dropping to the grass and jarring what felt like every bone and organ in his body. Doubled over, he managed to catch his breath and let the adrenaline take over. There would be some sort of alarm, Jake was sure of it. But if he could just get a slight head start...

He'd made it half-way up the trail when he heard a hearty laugh from the direction of the house. Looking to the side, he saw Abernathy leaning out of the window Jake had just vacated, waving.

"I'll join you presently," the man called, his tone cheerful. "Kate will be happy for the company, I'm quite certain."

Moving as fast as he could, Jake reached the apex of the hill and took in his surroundings. The cemetery was easy to find, given the clichéd white picket fence that had seen better days, and the tilted headstones trying valiantly to stand above it. Hobbling over the rough ground was slow going, considering his left leg wouldn't work quite right, and pain punctuated every step. When he finally reached the gate, it took him a few seconds to see the small bare foot sticking out from behind one of the large stones in back.

"Kate?" He swung the gate open and he hurried inside, tripping over the handle of a shovel and falling in a pile of freshly dug earth. Then he was sliding, his fingers clawing uselessly at the ground as gravity pulled him over a ledge and into a deep trench. He landed hard, blackness filling his vision as clumps of dirt rained down around him.

"Gotcha, you bastard." Kate's voice was the last thing he heard before he passed out.

* * *

It was dark, cold, and damp when Jake opened his eyes, and the blanket over him was too heavy. He tried to push it off with his arm, but the limb didn't seem to want to move. Starting to panic, he turned his head to the side and inhaled through his nose. A stale, musty dryness tickled the back of his throat and he coughed, dirt falling into his open mouth and absorbing what little saliva he had.

Then he remembered.

His heart raced as he squeezed his burning eyes shut, spitting out as much of the dirt as he could while he told himself to stay calm. It was an impossible task, with mud coating his tongue and the smell of dirt in his nostrils. All he could think about was how deep the hole was and how many feet of dirt could be on top of him that very second and how there was no air and no way to get air and he was going to suffocate and die in a hole dug by a half-crazed FBI agent he couldn't even remember sleeping with all because of a maniac he'd counseled too many years ago.

Full-on panic mode set in, and he fought to move his arms, his legs, his hands, but nothing would budge. Managing to wiggle one finger, he moved it around in ever-widening circles, but they kept collapsing, and after just a few seconds he gave up. The weight on his chest pressed down harder with every moment, and merely taking a shallow breath seemed like too much effort.

Acceptance seeped into his pores, and he relaxed as his mind grew fuzzy. There was an odd, muffled sound coming from...somewhere, teasing at what was left of his consciousness. He ignored it, drifting deeper into a peaceful white fog.

"Jake? Can you hear me?"

A sharp pain lanced through his left forearm, jolting him back to cruel reality. Instinctively trying to pull his arm close to his body, he was surprised when it responded almost immediately. As it swung upwards, he felt it break free of the earth's grasp, and small, ice-cold fingers wrapped around his.

"Thank God." Kate's voice was muffled through the layers of dirt, but she pulled hard on his arm. Realizing he wasn't going to die, Jake fought his way up through the dirt with her help and gulped air, coughing as tiny particles were sucked into his lungs.

"Glad you could join us again, Dr. Abernathy. I'm afraid I have to apologize - I assumed your colleague would be unconscious much longer than she was. I really must fix that little problem."

Jake looked up, squinting through stinging eyes at the blurry figure standing high above. The hole was much deeper than he would have guessed, and the need to get out was overwhelming. He clawed at the dirt walls, scrabbling to find some sort of handhold. Abernathy laughed, and a second later a rope hit Jake's shoulder.

"Hurry please, Dr. Werner. I'm afraid we've wasted too much time already."

Jake grabbed the rope, nearly blacking out at the sharp pain in his side. He tried to pull himself up, but the pain was too much, and he stumbled backwards into Kate.

"Agent Paige, I do believe you'll need to help Dr. Werner a little. Considering you put him down there, I don't think that's too much to ask, do you?"

"It wouldn't be anyway," she muttered under her breath, just close enough for Jake to hear. He felt her hands at his waist, and even though he hated needing her help, the touch was comforting.

"Can you lower the rope more, so I can tie it around him?" she called up to Abernathy. Her voice was surprisingly steady, and Jake was impressed with her ability to be calm even after all she'd been through so far.

A thick coil of rope soared over the edge of the hole, just barely missing Jake's head. Kate caught it, and placed it under his arms, tying a slip knot in front.

"Can you hold on here with your good arm?" She indicated a spot just above the knot, and Jake grasped it with a nod. She sank to her knees and made a cradle with her hands, holding them in front of him. "Here, I'll give you a boost."

He shook his head. "No way. I'm too heavy." No way could her slight frame handle his weight. The rope stretched taut, and he looked up to see

Abernathy pulling hand over hand, barely straining. It was odd to think that the man was nearly lifting him without any help whatsoever. Then again, someone had to move all those corpses, and Jake was fairly certain this serial killer worked alone.

"Go on," Abernathy said, straining now as Jake's feet left the ground. "I don't lift many live bodies, so no telling how long I can hold you up, or how high. Take her help."

Reluctantly Jake put one muddy foot into Kate's small hands, and was surprised when she propelled him upwards a couple feet. Abernathy gave a yell and yanked him higher at the same time, and Jake flopped up over the edge of the hole, only his legs still hanging down.

More pain ran through his body as Abernathy grabbed his arm and hauled him the rest of the way out. Strong fingers untied the knot at his chest, and Jake lay back on the soft earth, trying to catch his breath.

"Come on," Abernathy said, kicking at Jake's thigh. "Get up. You two have cost me precious time already."

Jake slowly got to his feet, swaying a little as dizziness caught him off guard. A sticky wetness on his arm made him look down - his whole side was covered in blood.

Damn.

"Move it, Werner." Abernathy prodded him in the

shoulder, and Jake took a step forward then stopped. "Or maybe you'd rather skip the party, though I know Angela will be disappointed not to see you there..."

"What about Kate?"

Abernathy laughed, the sound chilling and cold. "She's dug her grave. Now she gets to die in it."

Chapter Fifteen

As Dr. Werner swayed in front of him, Trent considered just tossing him back into the ground with his FBI girlfriend. It was disappointing, really - he'd thought the psychologist was stronger than that. And he really wanted to see the man's reaction to Angela's transformation. It's what all these years of testing and research had been about. The long nights waiting until she fell asleep in her car, the lab work and chemical concoctions, Angel herself...

It deserved an audience, damn it!

"Come on, Werner. Either move it, or you can join Agent Paige down there. I need to get back, so you've got three seconds to decide. One...two..."

Werner held up his hand. "Fine, I'm going!" He took a careful step forward, then another, the staggering gait still far too slow for Trent's liking. Shaking his head, Trent took a few steps to the left and came back with a wheelbarrow, pressing the edge into Werner's knees.

"I'll drive," Trent said as Werner lost his balance and fell backwards into the bucket. "The rate you're going, we'll miss the whole thing, and that's unacceptable. Though if you'd just listened to me from the start..."

"I'm not in the habit of listening to killers," Werner said, shifting to hold his side tighter. Abernathy thought about protesting the label, but really, it wasn't untrue. He did kill people. Even if they were only people who didn't matter.

"You should try it sometime," he said, just to watch the man squirm. "It can be very cathartic. Killing people, I mean. But if you're going to go to the effort, you may as well learn taxidermy as well. There's nothing quite so satisfying as making something new from something old, don't you think."

Werner shook his head. "You're sick, Abernathy. You need help. And drugs. Lots of drugs."

"Oh come now, doctor." Trent stopped to rest at the top of the small hill that bordered the yard, noting with satisfaction the crowd starting to build on the front lawn with video cameras rolling. "The people I...ah, helped to an early demise were already lost. I merely helped them make something of themselves, so to speak." He chuckled as he grasped the handles and began the slow trek down the hill.

"Not all of them," Werner said, his tone too smug

for Trent's taste. "Megan had a lot of potential until you stole her eyes. She had a home and a good job, not to mention her scholastic ambitions. Now maybe she'll overcome this, and maybe not, but don't kid yourself. You didn't do her any favors."

Trent set the wheelbarrow down at the bottom of the hill, and walked around to look Werner in the eye. "You don't understand. I needed those eyes. The color was just so...they were like nothing I'd ever seen before. When she looked at me, it was the most incredible..." he raised his hands, unable to express in words what he felt. When he looked down again, Werner was waiting. Watching him with a focus that made Trent distinctly uncomfortable.

"Well, I don't expect you to understand, doctor, but Ms. Hunter's eyes were definitely her greatest asset. And the fact that they haven't deteriorated as all the others did only proves my point. I was meant to have them, to give them to someone else. Someone far more worthy." He sighed, then shook his head. "I'll leave you to find your own way out front, Dr. Werner. I trust you'll stay for the party. Now if you'll excuse me, I must see to Angela."

* * *

Jake watched Abernathy walk toward the house, his gut clenching with indecision. Somehow he knew that whatever had happened to Angela, it wasn't good.

158

And Kate was trapped in a grave, though fortunately it seemed solid enough not to collapse in on her. Abernathy had clearly lost whatever presence of mind he'd had even a couple days ago, if he thought Jake turning up out front where the press was gathering would go unnoticed. It was probably his best chance at getting help, though the thought of being the center of so much attention was nauseating.

He tried to sit up from his half-reclined position in the wheelbarrow, nearly toppling the whole thing over. The pain was almost numbing now, and he turned side to side, examining the ground around him. Choosing the left and resigning himself to yet more pain, he deliberately rocked far enough to pour himself rather ungracefully onto the grass.

A collective gasp rose from the crowd in front, and for a moment he thought maybe someone had seen or heard him. Between the accident and Abernathy's treatment, Jake knew he wasn't looking so hot. But when he looked up, there wasn't a soul in the area, and he realized that Abernathy must finally have revealed his big secret. Low murmurs rose in pitch until a cacophony of sound traveled on the cool evening air. Somehow Jake managed to get to his feet, and one step at a time he reached the house and peered around the front corner at the crowd. All eyes were transfixed on a balcony high above, and Jake looked up, catching only a glimpse of Abernathy with a woman in a long white gown at his side.

Jake went to the back of the house as fast as he could hobble and let himself in the back door. Standing at the bottom of the stairs, he took a deep breath, knowing it was going to hurt like hell. Placing one foot on the bottom step and using his good arm for balance, he took one step up at a time. When he finally reached the top, sweat was pouring off him in waves, and he wanted to sit down and close his eyes more than just about anything, But he kept going, pushing doors open to peer inside until he found the one with French doors at the other end of the room.

Energy surged through him as he saw Abernathy standing beside Angela, right next to the rail. He knew then what he had to do. What someone should have done a long time ago. Tightening his muscles, he took a few deep breaths and called upon every ounce of strength he had. Forcing his legs to move, he ran through the doors and hit Abernathy with his own body, sending the man soaring over the railing to land with a satisfying smack on the driveway below.

Holding onto the rail, Jake bent over, trying to catch his breath and deal with the crippling pain of impact. Sirens rose over the noise of the crowd below, and Jake finally looked up at Angela. Bile rose in his throat as the face of Abernathy's doll looked back at him, complete with Megan's now-glassy eyes. She stepped closer to the railing, and he reached out for her, his fingers barely skimming her scarred wrist.

That wasn't Angela's hand.

"Angela?" Jake stood up straight, the blood rushing from his head making the world spin. "It's horrible, I know, but we'll get you help. There are doctors..."

The creature shook her head, wincing as though the movement caused her pain. When she tried to open her mouth, Jake saw tiny black stitches stretched between them, and it was all he could do to keep the meager contents of his stomach down.

"I'm so sorry," he said, wishing there was something, anything he could do. As strong as he knew the human mind was, he wasn't sure there was any way she could ever get over what Abernathy had done to her. He watched as she laid her useless hands on the edge of the railing and leaned over, watching the people surrounding her creator below. Jake knew he should go to her, pull her back from the edge and keep her safe.

Instead, he just watched as she slipped quietly over the edge.

Chapter Sixteen

Two weeks later, Jake cursed when the doorbell rang. Carefully easing up off the couch, he hobbled to the door, his injuries healing but not quite ready for normal activity. Checking the side window, he pulled open the door.

"Kate."

She nodded, unsmiling. "Can I come in?"

He moved aside and she stepped past him, her shoulders a little less straight than normal. He hadn't seen her since the day at Abernathy's, except for a few awkward visits in the hospital. Their relationship, if you could call it that, had been odd from the get go, and he'd assumed that after the case was closed, they'd go their separate ways. He followed her into the living room, making a detour to the kitchen for a couple of beers. She didn't argue when he handed her one of the bottles.

"Everything wrapped up with the case?" he asked,

162

figuring that was a good place to start.

She took a long swig of her beer, then nodded. "Abernathy was one sick individual, but you knew that. We found most of the stuff he cleared out of the mansion at the cabin, and with some poking around, the forensics crew found a secret room in the basement of the mansion with enough evidence to tie up a lot of older crimes, some going years back." She shook her head, staring absently at her fingernails. "It turns out Angela was his target all along. When he kidnapped her the first time, he did some sort of weird hypnotic stuff with her - we found some tapes at the house. That's why she was so obsessed with him. She literally couldn't get him out of her head. He wanted to create the ideal human, I guess, and she was the prototype." Kate took another swallow and shrugged. "It's over now, thanks to you."

It was Jake's turn to shrug. "Not really. It wasn't a one-person job, you know that." He leaned back in his chair. "So that's it then, I guess. Case is wrapped up and you're on to the next one."

She met his eyes with a slight nod. "I wanted to ask how Megan is. I went by the hospital, but they said she went home. I thought maybe you..."

"She's doing really well." Jake took a brochure off the coffee table and handed it to her. "As it turns out, Abernathy must really have felt bad about letting her live, because he set up a trust account in her name at that sight center. It took a little convincing, but she's there now, learning how to live without her sight." He hesitated, then decided to take a risk. "I'm going up to see her next week. You're welcome to come along if you want."

The silence hung thick between them, and he almost wished he hadn't asked, but she slowly nodded. "Thanks. I think I will."

Jake took a drink, knowing there was something else, but not sure what. He waited, fascinated by the tiny changes in Kate's expression before she finally spoke again.

"I...um...don't know if you're interested, but I have this case." She pulled up a document on what looked like a brand new tablet computer, and set it on the table between them. "If you're not too busy, I thought maybe you could tell me what you think. The department will pay a consultant's fee, of course."

Sitting forward, Jake propped his elbows on his knees and slid the tablet closer so he could look. "This is the crime scene?"

She nodded, some life coming back to her eyes. "We think someone's using a trained animal as a murder weapon. The trick is figuring out who...and what kind of animal. It's pretty gruesome, but we could use someone with your background to help us figure this out..."

Jake considered the offer for about two seconds, then looked up, meeting her cautiously hopeful stare.

"I'm in."

About the Author

Alex Westhaven is the pseudonym of an author from Billings, Montana. She resides there with her husband and two over-sized lap dogs. Halloween is her favorite holiday, and she has more than her fair share of skeletons (and other body parts) in the closet.

For information on upcoming books, visit AlexWesthaven.com.